the list assist

lynda tomalin

Cover Design by Jennifer Rackham
Editing and proofreading by Patricia Bell (www.bellbirdwords.com)

For everyone who's ever felt they've needed to hide a part of themselves

author note

While this is a sweet, fun story some subject matter may be upsetting for some readers.

This book contains descriptions of mental health struggles, in particular anxiety and grief.

There are also references to a teenager dying of cancer (off page, in the past) and minor injury by fire.

If you are concerned about any of the content of the book and would like more information, please reach out.

Recommended for readers aged 12+

to do list

- ❀ Stay out all night
- ❀ Dye my hair
- ❀ Go to an arcade
- ❀ Go bowling
- ❀ Go to a concert
- ❀ Spontaneous Swimming
- ❀ Meet a favourite author
- ❀ Get a tattoo
- ❀ A perfect first kiss under the stars
- ❀ Learn to dance
- ❀ Go on a road trip
- ❀ Celebrate with fireworks
- ❀ Cry from laughing too hard
- ❀ Break the rules
- ❀ Have an all day or night movie marathon
- ❀ Write a book
- ❀ Figure out who I am

THEY CANNOT ACTUALLY EXPECT me to sleep in this heinous excuse for a bedroom.

Can they?

I drop my bags on the floor and glare around.

My new room.

It's temporary, but the next couple of months are going to be torture in this place.

There's a lace curtain across the window and a floral blanket spread neatly across the bed, the corners perfectly square, the edges aligned with precision.

I unsling another bag from across my chest and toss it at the bed, hoping to hide the hideous blanket.

I take in the doll sitting on the shelf. Nope. No way. That's the first thing that's got to go.

"Rhett!" My grandfather's voice booms down the hall before I have a chance to stuff the creepy little doll into the cupboard or a drawer, or throw it out the window.

"Coming," I shout back, giving the lace curtain a final scowl before stomping back down the hallway.

"Your shoes can go by the door," Grandad says with a pointed look as I re-enter the living room.

I slide my feet out of the boots and set them near the front door next to Grandad's plain brown lace-ups and my grandmother's sandals, which are practical but also somehow … pretty.

Their choice in footwear pretty much sums up my grandparents.

Grandad is boring, plain, utilitarian.

Grandma is practical but still nice. Well, nice enough. We'll see how nice she is to me once I'm living under her roof.

"Take a seat." Grandad indicates the chair across from him at the table and I slide into it as Grandma places a plate of cookies and a glass of chocolate milk in front of me … like I'm six. I scowl, but pick up the glass and take a sip because it's chocolate milk and it's my favourite.

I place the glass carefully back on its coaster and lift my gaze to meet my grandfather's steely grey eyes—the eyes I inherited from my mother. I fight the urge to scowl again.

"We need to set some ground rules," he says.

"Yeah, sure," I reply, reaching for a cookie. They're still warm from the oven.

"First of all, you're to make sure you're at school, in class, when you're supposed to be. You're not to be out past 7 pm, and we need to know where you're going and who with if you're going anywhere but school or helping your grandmother."

I fight another urge, this time to roll my eyes. More rules than at home—typical. Though maybe if Mum and Dad hadn't been about to get on a plane for a two-month trip for Dad's job when I screwed everything up, maybe they'd have enforced some extra rules too.

Grandad is still talking and I struggle to tune back into what he's saying.

"Wait, what?"

"You're going to be helping your grandmother with the charity book fair," Grandad says, exasperation clear in his voice.

"Um, no." There is no way I'm spending my free time sorting through dusty old books with even dustier old people.

"It's non-negotiable," Grandad says, his voice firm, and I know he's not going to cave. But I'm not ready to yet either.

"Why?" I'm being belligerent and I really shouldn't be, but I also shouldn't even be here. I was supposed to be staying at home while my parents went on their trip, with only the occasional check-in with my grandparents. I'm old enough to take care of myself. My mother said it herself when they first made the plans.

But then I screwed everything up and now I have to be treated like a kid again.

"To go some way towards making reparations for what you did."

Oof. Can't really argue with that when he's so blunt about it.

"You keep your head down," he carries on. "Follow the rules, help with the book fair, and your mother has agreed that will go a long way towards paying for the damage you caused. Unless, of course, you'd like to pay for it yourself." He leans back in his chair and folds his arms across his chest. He's won and he knows it.

"Fine," I mutter. I'll do it, but it doesn't mean I'm going to be happy about it. Unfortunately, paying for it myself isn't really an option since I don't currently have a job.

"Go unpack and get settled in," Grandma says, reaching over and rubbing my shoulder. I want to lean into the touch, lean right over and let her wrap her arms around me like she used to do when I was little and had scraped my knees coming off a skateboard on their driveway.

But I'm eighteen now, and while hugs with their grandma might be some guy's jam, it's not mine. Not anymore.

I drain the last of the chocolate milk and push back from the table. I catch the pointed look Grandad gives the glass and plate, so I pick them up, heading for the kitchen.

I was intending to put them in the dishwasher without his reminder. I'm not a complete animal.

Once upon a time I was trusted to live by myself for two months.

Back in the hideous bedroom I unpack my clothes, shoving them roughly into the dresser drawers. I hang a couple of shirts and jackets in the wardrobe. My fingers linger on one jacket, and though I keep promising myself I'm going to stop, I slide it off the hanger again.

I wrap it around my fists, holding the soft, worn denim against my face, then after a few deep inhales I slip my arms into the sleeves.

I finish unpacking and then I pull out the battered paperback from the school library that I've been carrying around for the past two weeks. It has to be returned tomorrow, but I'm not done with it. I'll never be done with it.

I flop onto the bed and begin to read, opening the book to a random page. It doesn't matter; I know the story inside out by now.

After minutes, or hours, my eyelids begin to droop.

I wake the next morning sprawled across the floral blanket, the paperback on the floor beside the bed, still wearing that stupid jacket. Then I cry a few more tears into the fabric.

I LOVE the library first thing on a Monday morning, especially on a day like today. The sunlight filters in from the high windows, illuminating the rows and rows of books, all ready and waiting to take me away to another place and time.

It's also quiet. Really, really quiet.

There's no hallway rugby game going on with me constantly on edge, expecting to be hit in the head with a ball at any second. No rowdy groups recapping the weekend's events and loudly discussing who hooked up with whom and judging those of us who didn't go out and get wasted.

I release the catch on the returns box and stack the books onto a cart. There's always a rush of books returned on a Monday morning, probably because parents made their kids clean their rooms and they found all the outstanding books. I swipe the books back into the system, giving them a quick check-over for damage, and put a couple of ratty paperbacks that need some TLC to the side.

Restacking the books on the cart, I head into the stacks, the wheels whispering against the carpet. The only other sounds are those of my shoes brushing the floor and my breath, loud in my ears.

As I slip each book back onto its shelf, I wonder who checked it out and what they thought of it. I trail my finger down the spine of a Brigid Kemmerer book as I slide it into place beside the rest of its series. A Lynette Noni book goes home next. Fantasy is obviously big with whoever had these returns.

I round the end of the aisle and turn down the next one, heading for the R section.

I stumble over my own feet as the person standing in the middle of the row startles me. I didn't know anyone else was in the library, except for the actual librarian, Mrs Barrington.

This person—this guy—must have arrived before me. When I realise who it is I realise why. He probably doesn't want his stoner friends to find out he knows how to read, let alone visits a library.

His hand flashes out and grabs onto the cart, stopping it from crashing straight into him.

His name comes to me. Rhett. Rhett … something.

I don't even know his last name, even though we've shared the same classes in previous years. I don't think I've ever spoken to him before. He's not the sort of person I'm going to hang out with. His last name is something I'm quite happy never learning.

Rhett is glaring at the shelf like it's personally wronged him and he's planning some cold-blooded revenge.

His eyes flick to me, travel down to the ground, taking in my black pants and the oversized soft pink cardigan I'm wearing, and then back up.

Our eyes meet. He scowls. My breath catches and the words I was about to speak lodge in my throat.

He turns away, dismissing me in an instant. He doesn't move away though, and he's standing right where I need to get to. He studies the shelf for another long moment, his brow furrowing further with each passing second.

I stand there dumbly and stare at him. Eventually, the blockage in my throat clears and I'm able to speak again.

"Can I help you?" The words come out raspy, barely more than a whisper. I wish they hadn't. I wish they'd been clear and direct, and that it didn't sound like I was scared he was going to crush me like a bug under his shoe.

I glance down. Not even normal shoes. Big, black boots. I swallow and lift my gaze again.

He smirks down at me. "No," he says, drawing out the single syllable as his eyes roam over me again. I push my glasses up my nose with the tip of my finger. "I don't think you can help me with anything, sweetheart."

My skin prickles and I really wish I was the kind of person who'd fight back. The kind of person who'd reach out and slap the smug look off his face. At the very least I wish I could roll my eyes and act like his dismissive tone and total attitude problem don't feel like a personal attack.

He does step back though, leaning against the shelf on the other side of the aisle. He crosses an ankle over the other, then folds his arms against his chest. The denim jacket he's wearing pulls tight across his shoulders as he does, and he shrugs to adjust the fabric. The sleeves are a tiny bit short, and I realise that the jacket is too small for him. An interesting observation.

Then I push the thought out of my head and step forward, sliding the Percy Jackson book in my hand onto the shelf. The next two books in the series, the final two, aren't shelved. Disappointing for whoever just returned it.

I turn back to my cart and realise Rhett is still watching me.

"Do you need help finding something?" I ask, my voice less raspy this time, but still way too soft.

"No," he says as he gestures to the shelf. "What I want isn't there." He says it with such an edge to his voice that I wonder if I've unknowingly offended him in some way.

Our paths rarely cross; we don't exactly have a lot in common to draw us together, so I don't know how I could have offended him to such a degree.

"I can check when the books you want are due back," I say in a rush. Rhett clenches his jaw. "Are you after the—"

He cuts me off. "I've already told you, sweetheart," he says, stepping close. Way too close. I tilt my head back to look at him as his stormy grey eyes glare down at me. "You can't help me."

Then he steps around me, barely leaving enough space, though at least he doesn't push right past me. One shove from him and I'd likely go flying, what with all his coiled rage and all.

He disappears around the corner of the stacks and I'm left alone, surrounded by my favourite things, my hands shaking on the book cart.

"No need to be such a jerk," I mutter under my breath, and continue shelving the morning's returns.

rhett

I'M STARTING to think this girl is stalking me. Since the moment in the library this morning, when she almost ran her little book cart into me, I've been seeing her everywhere.

Across the hall from my English class, in the science block as I head for physics, sitting under a tree at lunchtime, her blonde ponytail falling over her shoulder as she buries her nose in a book.

So, since it's me seeing her all the time, I guess it's probably more like I'm stalking her.

But I'm suddenly seeing her everywhere I go and I don't know why. I know she's not new. She's vaguely familiar, she was too settled in her role of librarian and she's never looked confused or disorientated any other time I've seen her.

But how have I not paid her any attention before? Especially with my frequent trips to the library, although it's not like I linger there. I get in and out as fast as I possibly can.

But I'm not even in school right now and suddenly there she is. Again.

She's kneeling on the floor, surrounded by stacks of books she's sorting through. She's ditched her pink cardigan—which was so oversized and fuzzy she'd looked like she was wearing a blanket—and her shoes. She places a book on a pile, pushes her glasses up her nose and smiles up at an older woman who says something as she passes.

The girl laughs, and it startles me. After our encounter in the library this morning I assumed laughing wasn't part of this girl's day. She looked so serious, her lips turned down at the corners and brow furrowed the entire conversation.

Maybe she looked a little terrified too, so her lack of laughing was probably more to do with me than her. I don't like the feeling that thought creates inside my chest.

"Rhett," Grandma says, arriving at my side and tearing my attention away from the blonde. "You made it."

Well, yeah. I was told to be here at 3.45, so here I am.

Three forty-five on the dot. Not a minute sooner. I don't think Grandad realised I could have been here at 3.30 without any trouble, but I wasn't going to bring that titbit of information to his attention. For all I know, those fifteen minutes each afternoon are going to be the only freedom I get for the foreseeable future.

Grandma reaches out for me, maybe like she's going to hug me, but then rubs a hand over my shoulder.

"Right, where do you want to start?" she asks me.

I stare around the old warehouse we're in. Boxes and boxes of books are stacked at one end. At the other end and through the middle of the huge space are more boxes, interspersed with teetering stacks of books. These piles are separated, looking slightly more organised that the first stack of boxes, though I can't tell any more than that.

I survey the room. Several other people are here, slowly sorting through piles. My eyes land on the girl again as she stands, slips her sandals back on her feet and stoops to pick up a pile she's sorted, carrying it to one of the organised piles. As she turns back around, she's facing in my direction. She scans right past me, then her gaze flickers back to me for a second before she rips it away and spins to collect another pile of books. She looks so flustered it makes me want to smile.

"Oh good, Pat, you've brought some muscle," a new voice says, and I pull my attention away from the girl to see the woman who made her laugh standing beside my grandma.

"This is my grandson, Rhett," Grandma says, and the other woman holds out her hand.

"I'm Tonya," she says as I tentatively take her hand in mine. She's not as old as my grandparents; probably closer in age to my parents. She's got curly brown hair and is dressed casually, but far, far cooler than my parents could ever pull off, in slouchy jeans and an oversized shirt. "Glad to have your help. We're going to need it. This lot ain't much for heavy lifting and these books aren't exactly feathers." She gestures to the few other people in the room who are all older than her, probably older than Grandma, with several looking way more frail. Except of course for the girl, who I already know is my age, or at least close to it.

"Well, we may as well keep him busy, right Tonya?" Grandma says. "Where should we get him to start?"

"He could bring Sophie another box. She's almost done with the one she's been working through." Tonya gestures to me and I fall into step beside her with a glance towards Grandma, who gives me an encouraging little wave. "It's a matter of just finding something to do around here. But if you're able to do some of the heavy lifting that would be great. If there's none of that to do, Sophie can show you how we're sorting the books at the moment, which is pretty much into very wide genres."

"Well," I say, clearing my throat. "I don't really know much about books, so I don't know how much help I'll actually be."

Tonya scoffs. "You'll be fine. Trust me, you've got to have more brains in your head than some of these fools. Trevor!" She calls to a man nearby who's placed a book into a bag at his feet. "You're not supposed to be refilling your own shelves just yet, mate."

"Sorry, Tonya," he mutters, and slides the book back onto the table he's working at.

"See?" she says to me. "At least I shouldn't have to worry about you stealing the books meant for raising money for charity." She rolls her eyes and indicates the pile of boxes we've arrived at.

I pick one up. It's far heavier than I expect and I grunt with surprise. Tonya laughs and leads me back across the room. I'm expecting her to lead me to one of the grey-haired women to the right. But she doesn't. She leads me right to the blonde girl.

"Pat brought us some muscle," Tonya says with a laugh. The girl gives a small smile. "You can show him the ropes, yeah? Rhett, this is my niece, Sophie. I'll leave you in her more than capable hands."

Sophie. Her name echoes around my head.

I lift my gaze to meet hers and I can't tell what emotion I'm seeing there. I can't even tell if it's positive or negative.

"Hi," she says, her voice soft and gentle. Sweet. Like this morning when she offered to help me and I bit her head off. God, I think I called her sweetheart, and not in an endearing way. I remember the way it made her cheeks flush though, and I want to see that again.

I lift an eyebrow at her and feel my lip curling. "Hey." I lift my chin. "Where do you want this …" I indicate the box as I let my words trail off, then before I can think better of it I add "… sweetheart?"

4 /
sophie

WHATEVER I DID to deserve this ... I'm sorry.

I force myself to meet Rhett's steely grey eyes. It lasts barely a second before I have to look away.

"Over there," I murmur, indicating a spot on the floor where I want the box.

I turn, looking for Tonya, trying to find the words to get me out of showing him the ropes. But she's already gone, calling across the warehouse to someone who's leaving for the day.

I let out a sigh. Looks like I'm stuck with him.

Rhett sets the box on the floor and straightens, brushing his hands on his black jeans. He's not wearing the denim jacket anymore and his grey t-shirt shows off tanned forearms. I try not to notice his hands, his arms, his ridiculously annoying smirk.

I sink to the floor, ignoring him, and start unpacking the box, creating new piles depending on what I pull out. Adult fiction, children's fiction, non-fiction, recipe books.

"What do you want me to do?" Rhett asks, crossing his arms and shifting from foot to foot. He goes to lean against a nearby table and realises at the last moment it's not stable enough to hold his weight. He stumbles slightly as it slides away from him, then straightens and folds his arms across his chest. A moment later he uncrosses them and tucks his hands in his pockets. If I didn't know any better I'd think he was nervous, or at the very least, uncomfortable.

I shrug. "Go lift a box for someone else, I suppose." I wish I could say the words that are in my head. I wish I could tell him I can't help him, like he said to me this morning with a sneer.

But I'm useless at any kind of confrontation, at sticking up for myself. It's easier to fade into the background, avoid drawing attention to myself.

"Trish looks like she's done with hers," I say, inwardly scowling at myself as I do. I wave towards the woman, who must be in her eighties.

Rhett grunts and heads towards the stack of unsorted boxes, then heads towards Trish, depositing the box beside her. Trish glances up and says something to him with a smile, and I'm shocked to my core when Rhett smiles back.

I stare at the expression on his face and immediately want to know what Trish said to cause it.

Wait a minute, no I don't. I shove that thought away. I don't care why Rhett is smiling. I'm only startled because I've never seen it happen before. Yeah, he's smirked at me, glared and glowered at teachers. But I've never seen that look on his face.

The thing is, Trish isn't even *nice*. She's sour and bitter and spends any time I'm around criticising and complaining about everything from her morning cup of tea to the way the news reporter on the radio pronounced something.

She isn't one to smile, either.

Maybe it's that they're two grouchy people coming together. They've found common ground.

Rhett glances my way and catches me staring. I start and turn away, back to my own box of books.

Adult fiction, adult fiction, adult fiction. I stack book after book with bleak covers into the pile.

Another box is placed gently beside me before Rhett folds himself into a pretzel on the floor next to it.

"So, just sort them into types of books?" he asks.

"Yeah, pretty much," I say, barely containing my sigh. Why did he have to come and sit here? Why couldn't he have stayed with Trish?

We work in silence and I keep myself turned away from him as much as possible. I don't want to talk to him. I don't even know why he's near me. I don't know why he's here at all.

"So," he says, finally breaking the silence. "What're you in here for?"

"Excuse me?" I finally turn to look at him, twisting around as I place a recipe book on the pile closest to him.

"What'd you do …" he trails off, studying me closely. "Oh, no. Please tell me you aren't here by *choice*."

I feel my face flush hot. Because yeah, obviously I'm here volunteering my time of my own free will.

I open my mouth to speak, but nothing comes out so I snap it closed again.

"Of course." Rhett glances around the room, surveying the selection of people here, the stacks and stacks of books. "Spend your mornings in the library and your afternoons here, huh? I shouldn't be surprised."

I shrug, hoping the heat in my cheeks isn't as visible as it feels and that my gesture looks nonchalant. "I like helping and I like the books. If you're so shocked by my choice to be here, then why are you here?"

He's been staring at me with this look of incredulity on his face, his eyes narrowed in a way that makes him look like he's trying to work out a puzzle, and chewing his bottom lip. "I don't think you're ready for that story, sweetheart," he says.

I sigh audibly and turn back to my box of books. "Sort your books and leave me alone."

That seems to stun him into silence for a moment. "I feel like we got off on the wrong foot," he says eventually.

I say nothing.

"I'm Rhett," he says and I see his hand extend into my peripheral vision, like he wants me to shake it.

"I know who you are."

"Oh, my reputation precedes me." He grins and quirks an eyebrow.

I take a deep breath, scoop up a stack of books and stand. "I wouldn't sound so happy about it. It's nothing good."

Then I walk away.

I want *desperately* to glance over my shoulder and see the expression on his face. I fight the urge and win, but barely.

I've never said anything like that in my life. Not out loud. To an actual person. To the person I'm saying it about.

I feel stupidly proud, but I realise I'm shaking as I try to deposit my pile on the table reserved for picture books.

I'm fortifying myself for the return trip, for having to face Rhett and his self-satisfied attitude again when Tonya saves me from myself.

"Soph, honey, come here," she calls across the room. I glance towards Rhett, who's watching me as he places a book on a pile. Our eyes lock and he misses his mark, dropping the book on the floor instead.

I roll my eyes, covering it up by pushing my glasses up my nose, then head towards my aunt.

"Look what I found," she says, holding up a complete, virtually new-looking box set.

"Ooh," I breathe as I reach out and run a finger down the spines.

"Do you want me to set it aside for you?"

I shake my head. "I already have that series. And besides, what's this 'setting it aside'? You're constantly telling Trevor he's not allowed to take books."

"Yeah, but Trevor's barely helpful—even when he's not restocking his own library. Plus, I meant I can set it aside for you with that signed Tobias Madden hardcover over there and you can buy them later. We'd better send some money into the till or you'll be *worse* than Trevor."

I gasp at her mention of the book, then laugh. She's right. If I had free rein in this place there'd barely be anything left to sell to the public. "This is true. Can I see the book?"

She laughs and pulls it from behind a stack.

I marvel at it. One of my favourites. I mean, I have many favourites, but I do love this one. It was never released here in hardcover so it's a rare find. And *signed*.

"We'll put a box over here with your name on it. Put anything you want in there and we can decide at the end how much you'll pay for them, okay?"

"This is a very, very dangerous situation," I say.

"I know, but we must all take risks once or twice," she says, wrapping an arm around my shoulder and plucking the book from my fingers. She places it into the box, then shoos me back to my task.

I'M FINALLY ALLOWED to leave the book sorting warehouse at five, when Grandma asks me to take her home. Grandad must have dropped her off earlier, and since she no longer drives it's apparently up to me to get her home again.

"It wasn't so bad, was it?" Grandma asks as I flop into my car seat with a heavy sigh.

"Nah, it wasn't too bad," I say, mostly to reassure her. The endless sorting bored me to tears but it wasn't hard, and if this is what I have to do to redeem myself, or at least pay off the damage, then I'll do it.

"I know you don't want to be there," Grandma says as she smiles across the car at me. "But at least there's someone else your age."

I think of Sophie and the way I caught her staring at me as I spoke to Trish, then about how she told me nothing she knew about me was good. I wonder what she's heard about me, or if she's formed her own opinions based on my behaviour this morning.

"Yeah, I'm not sure I'm ever going to be one of Sophie's favourite people," I say.

Grandma sighs and I think I've disappointed her again, but then a laugh bursts out of her. She tries to stifle it but fails spectacularly as she snorts. "You've already annoyed her? What'd you do? She's a sweetheart."

I snort at her choice of word. "Exactly," I say through my own laughter as I turn into my grandparents' street. "But I don't think she appreciated it when I called her that."

That sets Grandma off again.

I pull into the driveway, put the car in park and rest my head against the steering wheel. Laughter wheezes out of me as I recall her face each time I threw the endearment her way.

Eventually the laughter subsides, and I realise Grandma is watching me, her features soft and wistful.

"It's nice to see you laughing again," she says, reaching out and resting her hand on my shoulder. "We haven't seen much of it since Dusty..." Her voice trails off as she says his name and my chest constricts in that same instant.

My good mood evaporates in a millisecond.

"I'm sorry," I whisper, the crushing weight of devastation settling across my shoulders again. It had been a blissful moment when it lifted, but now the hollow ache is back in my chest at the reminder of what I lost, at what that loss caused me to do.

"Oh, Rhett, honey, you don't need to apologise. I know it hasn't been easy on you."

"I'm sorry I've caused so much trouble." Tears burn at my eyes. I can't look at her as I say the next words. "Grandad, and everyone else, is so angry with me."

"He's not angry. None of us are. We're worried about you."

I glance over, disbelief threading through me as I shake my head. "Yeah, sure," I mutter. He seems pretty angry for someone who's worried about me. I've always admired my grandad, always looked up to him and feeling like I've let him—and everyone else—down makes this whole situation even worse.

Grandma looks like she's going to argue the point, but I cut her off. "Anyway, I'm sorry. I'll do whatever I need to make up for everything."

"I know you will, honey," Grandma says. "Can I suggest you maybe try to improve things with Sophie? You two will be spending a lot of time together until this book fair."

I groan. "Really? Her?"

"What's wrong with Sophie?" Grandma's voice finds the slightest edge, like I've offended her.

"There's nothing wrong with her exactly … she's just …" I really don't know what word to use here. "She doesn't seem like much fun."

Grandma sighs. "You're not exactly there to have fun, Rhett."

"I know, I know. But that's what she's doing for fun. Like, it's how she's choosing to spend her time. Doing that and being school librarian." I shrug. As soon as the words leave my mouth I realise how much of a jerk I'm being. Who am I to judge someone else for being no fun, anyway? It's not like I can talk.

But it's too late now.

"Because your kind of fun has worked out so well for you?"

Ooof. Shots fired. Grandma raises an eyebrow at me. "A change of pace might be good for you, Rhett. Sophie is a lovely girl and you might learn there's more to life than what you've been doing for the past few years."

Oh, she is peeved. "I know. I'm sorry, Grandma. I'll try."

"Good," she says, then climbs out of the car, leaving me sitting there wondering about all the different parts of that conversation.

Sophie and Dusty, and my Grandad apparently not being angry with me. Only worried. That's a puzzle for another day.

I drag myself inside, relief flooding through me when I realise Grandad isn't home.

"Do you need a hand with anything?" I ask Grandma, mostly because I know it's expected of me, rather than particularly wanting to be helpful.

"No, you're all good, honey. I assume you have homework to do. I'll call you when dinner is ready."

I nod my appreciation and head straight for my room. I still haven't adjusted to the floral-ness of it all. I suppose I could change it up a little bit, but it doesn't really feel worth it. At least there's a desk in here, albeit tiny, so I don't have to do my homework at the dining room table.

I settle down with my stack of books, but my brain refuses to focus on physics.

Grandma's mention of Dusty echoes through my mind and I find myself laying my head on my desk and thinking of my best friend.

Dusty was the best person. It's never made sense to me why the universe would give cancer to the greatest person I've ever known. Sixteen years old and his life was over. Not that he had much of a life those last few years. It was all fighting and treatments and getting sicker and sicker.

It's now been over a year since he died.

I remember it like it was yesterday.

I spent the day lying on the couch next to his bed that had been set up in his family living room. I watched five movies while Dusty mostly slept.

Mum picked me up at 8 pm and I squeezed his hand and told him I'd be back in the morning.

I was, but he wasn't there anymore.

Despite knowing it was coming, despite expecting it, it still felled me with brutal efficiency.

Dusty's mum phoned mine first thing in the morning and the moment I stumbled downstairs and saw the tears on her face as she sat at the kitchen table, I knew.

I knew that my best friend was gone and I'd never, ever be the same again.

sophie

"SOPHIE," my best friend Theo says as they drop onto the ground beside me. I'm sitting under our favourite tree, a paperback open in my lap.

"Yeah?" I glance up as they rearrange themselves into a cross-legged position, pulling an apple from their bag.

"Why is Rhett Carmichael *staring* at you?"

"What?" That cannot be right. Rhett. Ugh. "Don't be ridiculous."

"I'm offended by that," they tease. "I'm not ridiculous. And he is. Staring I mean, not ridiculous. Right over there." Theo waves to my left. "He is ridiculously hot though," they say as an afterthought.

I turn my head slowly. Rhett is sitting at a picnic table with a group of his friends and Theo is right. He's staring at me between the heads of the two people sitting with their backs to us.

His t-shirt today is dark blue. Always with the dark colours. Moody must be his aesthetic. I mean, he pulls it off well, but still. Nothing wrong with a bit of colour.

He doesn't break eye contact when I catch him staring. He

holds it. I feel my cheeks heating and Theo lets out a low whistle beside me.

"I so badly want to know what's going on with *that*," they say.

Then, right before I tear my gaze away because I feel like I'm going to spontaneously combust, Rhett flashes me a blinding grin. His entire face transforms for the space of a breath, before someone shunts him along the bench he's on and he's forced to look away.

I turn back to my book, picking it up from my lap and hoping Theo lets me disappear into it. I read in their company all the time; it's not like it's unusual or I'm being rude or anything.

"Oh, no. That's not happening." They snatch the book from my hands and grin at me. "Why was Rhett Carmichael staring at you? And more importantly, why did he *smile* at you?"

I tell them the truth. "I have no idea." I want to look at him again, to see if he's watching me, but I'm too scared. I don't know what it means if he is, or if he isn't.

"It's okay," Theo says. "He's not looking anymore." A pause. "Okay, there's the occasional glance. Soph, what is going on? I wouldn't have thought he'd even know who you are."

"Ouch. That was rude," I say, but I know exactly what Theo means, so there isn't any bite behind it. Just a soft, sad sort-of laugh. "He's helping with the book fair. I think against his will, but he was there yesterday with his grandma."

I think about telling Theo about yesterday morning in the library, then dismiss the thought. It doesn't matter, and I don't really want to think about it any more than I already have.

"So are you like, friends now?"

I laugh. "Me? Friends? With Rhett? No."

"That's not what his pretty grey eyes are telling me," Theo says.

"I didn't know you could look at someone's eyes and tell who their friends are. Can I have my book back yet?"

Theo assesses me, holding the book just far enough away that I'd have to lunge to get it. I contemplate doing it despite how ridiculous I'd look. "You are correct. Okay, Rhett's pretty grey eyes are telling me that he wants to be friends with you … or you know, something else." An elaborate eyebrow wiggle follows that statement. "Also, I like this snark on you. You must have got it from him. I should send a fruit basket."

"A fruit basket? What?"

"You're like, never snarky. And you have been to me, more than once in this single conversation. Since snark is my love language, I'm feeling very adored right now. And I'm so proud of you."

"I still don't get who you're sending a fruit basket to."

"Rhett. Obviously. Has he befuddled you with his whole moody boy look?"

I scowl at them, then my eyes stray towards where Rhett's group of friends is sitting. He's laughing, and again I'm struck dumb by how his face looks when he's not frowning at me.

Theo sighs. "I can only assume that your newly developed snark is a by-product of spending time near that boy. I highly recommend you continue." Then they toss my book back to me. I catch it awkwardly but manage to save it before my bookmark falls out and I spend the rest of lunchtime finding my place again.

Theo pulls their headphones on and I reopen the book.

I try to focus on the words as we settle into our usual companionable silence, but it's hard to concentrate with thoughts of Rhett and what Theo said swirling around in my brain.

WHEN THE BELL RINGS, I slide my book into my bag and climb to my feet. I fall into step beside Theo and head for our next class. As we pass the table where Rhett's friends are dispersing, my eyes are once again drawn towards him. He smiles when my gaze meets his, like he's been expecting it, waiting for it.

"Hey there … sweetheart," he calls to me, his eyes alight with mirth. "Theo," he says to my best friend with a casual nod.

"Rhett," Theo replies with the same solemnity.

I say nothing as my face flames. I flash a tight smile in Rhett's direction.

The second we're past him Theo gasps, their hand shooting out to grip my arm, fingernails digging into my skin. "He called you sweetheart!"

I roll my eyes. "It's not an endearment, Theo."

"Uh, yeah it is. My parents call each other that all the time." I look at them sideways. "Okay, so that's a poor example."

"He's mocking me. That's it. There's nothing going on, so let it go now, okay? Please."

"Well, I don't believe that. But I'll shut up about it … for now."

"Thank you," I say, knowing I sound stupidly prim and proper. I realise it's exactly that behaviour that gives someone like Rhett so many reasons to mock me.

We turn to head into the science building and a body skims past us right before we do.

I startle and pause to catch my breath.

"See you after school," Rhett's voice calls back to me as he disappears down the hallway. "I'm looking forward to it."

rhett

AS EXPECTED, Sophie beats me to the warehouse after school. I wonder how long it'll be before my grandparents realise if she can make it there so quickly, then I can too.

Or maybe Grandma won't mention it to Grandad and I'll get to keep my tiny slice of freedom.

I watch Sophie for a moment as she chats with a woman who wasn't here yesterday. She's holding a book in her hand, and the way she's gesturing to it I feel like she's giving it a rave review and trying to convince the other woman to read it.

"Oh, you're here. Great," Tonya says, coming to a stop beside me.

I tear my gaze from Sophie, hoping her aunt hasn't realised where I was looking. "Uh, yeah, great," I say, having to clear my throat.

"Are you okay to go with Soph today to do pick-ups?"

I glance back across the warehouse at Sophie. She's smiling at someone else now. Today she's wearing cut-off denim shorts with frayed edges and a mint green t-shirt that has little white flowers printed all over it. She almost looks like a typical teenager, which after yesterday's outfit is a little bit shocking.

Yesterday she looked like a librarian. Like a stereotypical old-lady librarian. All she needed was a pearl necklace. What teenage girl wears pants made of anything other than denim, fleece or lycra to school? Sophie, that's who, in her tailored dress pants and cardigan and glasses.

"Pick-ups?" I force myself to remember I'm supposed to be having a conversation with Tonya.

"We have a couple of drop-off points around town where people can donate their books. Can you go with Sophie to pick them up today?"

"Oh, yeah, sure. No problem. If she doesn't mind."

"Why would she mind?"

I shrug. "I feel like we didn't really get off on the right foot." I think about the way she scowled at me every time I called her sweetheart. I mean, calling her that at school, in front of Theo, probably wasn't the smartest move on my part.

But the way it makes her blush makes it irresistible.

Tonya laughs. "Sophie will be fine. She knows where to go, so I'll leave you in her capable hands again." She pats me on the shoulder and wanders off to collect a box for sorting.

I take a deep breath and fortify myself, preparing to face the fallout of calling Sophie sweetheart in public.

I stride across the room, but my steps falter as I get closer and she turns to face me, resting her brown eyes on my face.

Her brow pinches, and I try not to take it to heart.

"Hey, sweetheart." I grin at her, and right on cue the blush flares across her skin. She's so much fun. "I hear you get to enjoy the pleasure of my company this fine afternoon."

She sighs, pushes her glasses up her nose with a knuckle and tries to glare at me. I think. She squints at me and the corners of her mouth turn down, like she wants to be mad. Then it all smooths out with a sigh and she's completely amiable again. "Fine. Come on then."

She heads for the door, waving to Tonya as she goes, and I trail after her. I can't figure out if she hates me or not. She's so … ambivalent about me.

Not for the first time in the past year, I wish I could speak to Dusty about it. The pang of his loss hits me squarely in the chest like it always does, and I stumble over my own feet.

"You good?" Sophie has stopped next to a tiny blue hatchback and is watching me.

"Yeah, sure," I say, clearing away the blockage in my throat. "Are we taking this?" I look at the car, wondering how many boxes we can even fit in there.

"Yes, we are," she says. "What else would we take?"

"My car," I say, gesturing towards the black SUV. "Way more room. Probably a better stereo."

She studies me and the car, her serious gaze trailing over me from head to toe. I want to step away from it, but all I can do is pull my keys from my pocket and twirl them around my finger.

"I don't know if that's a—"

"Good idea?" I finish for her. "Why not? I can drive. Tonya knows where you're going and who with. Answer me honestly, will we be able to fit everything in your itty-bitty car? Or will we have to do multiple trips?"

She says nothing, but glances between the two vehicles. She's wavering.

"Come on, mine's way bigger. I promise I'm a good driver."

"Fine," she says, pocketing her keys again. She sounds defeated, and I wish I hadn't made her feel like that.

She heads straight for the passenger side of my car, and as I unlock the doors she climbs in immediately, reaching for the above door handle to pull herself up. She looks so tiny sitting there. I'm used to only carting around my giant, oafish friends.

I slide into my seat and start the ignition.

"It's a very nice car," she says, voice quiet.

"It's actually my mum's, but she's away at the moment. I figured I'd make the most of it while I could."

She smiles at me. It's soft, like the rest of her. Soft and quiet and barely noticeable. "Where is she?"

"My dad had to go on a trip for work and my mum went with him. They're in the States for two months."

"And that's how you ended up staying with your grandparents?"

I shrug. "Pretty much, yeah."

"How did you get stuck helping me?"

I stiffen at her words and glance over at her. She's staring steadily out the window like she hasn't just asked a really probing question. For someone like her, it probably isn't. She probably can't even imagine getting into trouble.

"Who says I'm stuck helping you?"

"You pretty much did yesterday. When you asked what I was in for, and indicated I had to be not-right-in-the-head to actually want to be here."

Oh, right. That conversation.

"And I told you that you weren't ready for that story. Are you *prying*?" I really didn't think she had it in her, so I'm pleasantly surprised, especially when her lip twitches up at my tone.

"No," she says, huffing out a breath. "I was merely trying to pass the time by making civil conversation. Would you rather we talked about the weather?"

Actually, yeah. I would.

8 /
sophie

I HAVE NEVER MET a person more confusing than Rhett Carmichael.

He's almost intoxicatingly charming, and can lure smiles out of even the grouchiest of volunteers at the book warehouse. He chats to them all like they've been friends for years. Then he speaks to me like we're besties, like we whisper secrets in the dark and laugh until we cry.

But when I ask why he's here helping, when it's clearly not his own choice to be, he shuts up like a clam.

He actually comments on the weather.

"Nice day, isn't it?" he says. "Good to have the sun out."

"Um, yeah, sure."

We fall into silence. I truly don't know what else to ask him. I know nothing about him, and if we hadn't been forced to spend this time together our paths would never have crossed.

"Where's the first stop?" He breaks the silence after a few moments, and I realise I haven't even told him the direction he's supposed to be driving. It's a coincidence that he's already going the right way.

"You know Oh, Sweet Bagels?"

"That café with those ridiculous donuts?"

"Yes. That's the first stop."

He groans. "You'll have to go in. I can't. I'll come out carrying more donuts than books."

"I'm sure you'll cope." I roll my eyes, but I'm sort of smiling at his dramatics.

"Uh, I'm pretty sure I won't. Here," he says as he hands me his phone. "Put something on."

I stare at him blankly, then realise his phone is open to his music. "What do you want to listen to?" I ask. My hands feel clammy, like I'm nervous.

He shrugs and glances over at me when he stops at an intersection. "Whatever you want."

I glance down at the screen and tap on his most recent playlist, hitting the play button.

Something that must be classed as a rock song comes through the car speakers and he lets out a bark of a laugh. "You picked whatever I last listened to, didn't you?"

"So? You said you didn't care what I chose."

Another intersection and another glance my way. "You're allowed to have an opinion."

I shrug. "I'm not that into music. It doesn't really matter."

Rhett shakes his head in this kind of sad way, and I wonder if he's somehow disappointed in me. I don't know why he'd care that much.

"Well, I do really love this song," he says after a moment of silence. "So I guess it's all right."

I stare out the window as we drive, enjoying the way the sun sparks off different surfaces and Rhett's low singing. I can't hear him well enough to actually make out the words, but it's definitely more than just humming. His voice is soft and rich and I let it wash over me.

Three songs later he pulls into a parking space right in front of the café, which is pretty much a miracle at this time of day.

I undo my seatbelt and reach for the door handle, then realise Rhett hasn't moved his hands from the steering wheel. He hasn't even put the car in park.

"Are you okay?" I ask, noticing the tense line of his body, the way his fists clench around the steering wheel.

He releases a shaky breath and clears his throat. "Ah, yeah. I, uh, just need a moment."

He uncurls his fingers and shifts the car into park, then switches off the ignition. He leans back in his seat and closes his eyes, taking long slow breaths as the current song ends and another begins. He reaches over and wrenches the cable connecting the phone to the car from the outlet, cutting off the song after a mere handful of beats.

I stay sitting in the front seat next to him, unsure if I'm supposed to be witnessing this or not. I pick at my fingernails and try to decide if I should get out of the car.

After a few more breaths Rhett opens his eyes and pins me with a single look. My hand is halfway across the space between my body and the door handle. "Sorry," he says, his voice low.

I drop my hand into my lap and rub my palms against the denim of my shorts. "Are you sure you're okay?"

He nods. "I really love that song, but it also sets me off sometimes." He rubs a hand across his face, dragging it along his jaw, his steely grey eyes never leaving mine as we stare at each other across the confines of the car. "Sorry."

"You don't have to keep apologising," I say. "It's okay."

"I'm not used to it happening in front of other people." He rubs his face again. "I don't really know what to say."

"Do you want to talk about why? Or anything? Or do you want me to pretend like this didn't happen?"

He gives me a half-hearted smile at that, and I feel myself relaxing slightly. It's such a shock to see Rhett emotional and unsure. I mean, I hardly know him, but so far in every interaction he's been so confident and self-assured. If he's smiling he must be doing better, and we can return to whatever equilibrium we've had before now.

"I think if we pretend it didn't happen?" He rubs his jaw again and I find myself following the movement. "I'd definitely appreciate it if you didn't tell anyone ..." he trails off, then gives me a sheepish smile. "If that's okay?"

"Yeah," I say, my voice soft. "It's none of my business, or anyone else's."

We fall into silence again and I turn to stare out the windscreen. After another long moment Rhett jerks in his seat.

"Right," he says, sitting up straight. "Okay. I'm good. You ready to go find some books?"

"Yes," I say, reaching for the door handle.

"If the pull of the donuts is too strong, save yourself and the books. I might not make it out."

I laugh. I'm startled by it, and also by the way Rhett has so quickly switched back to his usual self. He gives me a grin as he rounds the front of the car.

"They can't be *that* good," I say.

Rhett turns to me as his mouth slowly drops open. "You don't *know*? You've never tried them?" He's incredulous.

I shrug. "Not really my thing, I guess?"

"Well, that needs remedying immediately," he says, and swings open the door to the café. "My shout."

"You're only saying that so you can get one," I say, and I'm laughing again.

Rhett looks down at me, his eyes sparkling, a stark contrast to a few minutes ago in the car. "Maybe, maybe not. But it doesn't really matter. After one of these you'll never be the same again."

"Yeah, okay, sure. Life-changing donut." I roll my eyes and he grins.

"Look, sweetheart, if there is one thing I know, it's donuts. I'm proving this point, so go choose."

Then he places his fingers across my back and steers me towards the cabinet.

"HEY, SOPHIE," the guy behind the counter says with a smile as soon as she approaches. I know I've seen him around school, but I can't quite put a name to his face. Sean? Steve? I think it's an 'S' name.

"Oh, hey, Sam," she replies, shooting him a smile, but she's studying the contents of the cabinet like she's never even looked at it before.

"We've got a couple of boxes for you today," Sam says. "I can help you carry them out if you want."

"It's okay," Sophie says. She waves towards me, still distracted by the rows of donuts. "I brought some muscle with me."

Sam's face shifts ever so slightly as he glances at me, and I recognise the look of disappointment that flits across it before it reverts back to a smile—although this one is a little more forced than the hopeful one he was wearing a moment ago.

Sophie turns to me. "What's good?"

"They're all good. Like honestly, all of them. You can't go wrong."

"He's right," Sam adds, like he's fighting his way back into the conversation. I admire his commitment, especially when Sophie is so completely oblivious to his flirting. "The chocolate custard is my favourite."

I step up beside her to see what's on offer today. She turns to me and peers up, her brown eyes soft behind the frames of her glasses. "What's your favourite?"

I swallow. Clear my throat. "Uh, the caramel one. Or the white chocolate raspberry. Or the chocolate one."

Sophie's mouth curls up on one side. "So, all of them."

I smile back and groan comically. "Like I keep telling you. I don't know why you won't believe me."

She laughs. "That doesn't help me decide," she says, breaking our eye contact and freeing me from the spell she just cast. I don't know how she did it, but for a moment there I thought I'd lost my ability to speak.

"Why don't I put these books in the car while you decide?"

"I don't think more time is going to help," she says, but I'm already moving away to where Sam has pointed out the boxes of donated books, ready and waiting to go.

"Do you need a hand?" he asks me as I bend to pick up the first box.

Simultaneously our gazes flick to Sophie, then back to each other. "Nah, I'm good," I say, and a spark comes back into his eye. "Help her choose or we'll be here all day."

Sam laughs and gives my arm a light punch. "Thanks, man."

I carry the box to the car and slide it into the boot, then return for the next one. Three more trips later and I find Sophie at the counter, a box of donuts in front of her with one space left.

"I didn't know which one you wanted," she says, turning to me as I approach.

"It looks like you don't know which one you wanted either," I say, indicating the five donuts already in the box.

She blushes. "I'm going to share them," she says hotly.

"Sure, sweetheart. Whatever you say."

She reaches out and whacks at my arm, but she's smiling again.

"A boysenberry custard one, please," I say to Sam after surveying the box. "She shouldn't miss that one."

He slides the donut out of the cabinet and into the box, then presses some buttons on the till. I'm pulling my wallet out of my pocket when Sophie pulls her own out of the bag she's wearing slung across a shoulder. I hadn't even realised she had it with her.

"Oh, no!" She startles as several sheets of paper fly out of her bag along with the wallet. They drift to the floor around her. Before attempting to pick them up she turns to Sam, holding out a card.

"No, I said it was my shout," I say, reaching over and sliding my card onto the counter.

"Yeah, but then I got five." She crouches and shuffles a few sheets of paper together.

I bend down and snatch up the few closest to me. "Doesn't matter. I didn't put a limit on it." I turn to Sam. "I'll pay." He nods at me, and I slide my card into the machine.

Sophie stands, stuffing the sheets of paper back into her bag. "Well, thank you," she says, somewhat begrudgingly, like I'm forcing donuts upon her.

"No worries, sweetheart," I say with a grin, and she scowls but picks up the box and follows me from the café, calling a farewell to Sam on the way.

"What's all this?" I ask, coming to an abrupt halt on the foot-path beside the car as I realise the pages I hold in my hand are covered in lists, in what I can only assume is Sophie's soft, almost cursive handwriting. She's drawn little flowers and hearts around the edges of the pages and the words "To Do List" are coloured in across the top of the one uppermost in my hand.

The first item listed is "Stay out all night". The second is "Dye my hair". I think I catch the words "tattoo" and "kiss" before the pages are ripped from my grasp.

Sophie clasps them to her chest with one hand, the other barely balancing the teetering donut box. Her cheeks are flushed a deep pink and her eyes look kind of wild.

She stares at me for several long moments, saying nothing until I reach out and gently take the box from her hand.

"It's nothing," she says abruptly.

I know that's not true, but she gave me grace for my meltdown in the car over Dusty's favourite song, the one they played at his funeral as I helped carry his casket out of the building, so I'm going to give her grace now.

"Okay," I say, and hit the button to unlock the car doors.

I walk around to the driver's door and climb in. By the time I do Sophie's already in her seat, shoving the papers inside her bag and snapping it closed.

"How much did you read?" she asks, her voice wary.

"Nothing," I say.

She scowls at me.

"Okay, so a little bit. Like two lines. But it's fine, it's not any of my business, or anyone else's." I repeat her reassuring words back to her, hoping that they'll work for her like they did for me.

She watches me for a long moment, the sunlight reflecting off the frames of her glasses so it's difficult for me to see whatever emotion is playing out in her eyes. "Okay," she says eventually, her voice quiet and a little shaky.

"Right," I say, as I start the car and shift it into drive. "Now I'll show you the absolute best place to eat donuts." I indicate and pull onto the road, turning right at the end and heading for my favourite spot ever.

10 /
sophie

I GRIP the box of donuts in my lap and wonder what two lines Rhett could have read on the papers that fell out of my bag.

Of course they weren't simply notes from biology. Nope, they were the pages I wanted to carry over from my old journal, which I completely filled two nights ago.

I ripped a few pages out, the ones I constantly refer to, ready to glue them into the new journal, which is all fresh pages and endless possibilities.

I shudder to think what Rhett read, but it doesn't seem like he's going to use whatever information he gleaned against me. Yet anyway.

"Where are we going?" I ask, when it's clear he has no interest in visiting the next book donation location.

"The best place ever," he says, shooting a grin in my direction. He turns onto the road leading up to the lookout with views over the coast. It's a narrow, winding road to the top, and as Rhett pulls over to allow a car heading down the hill to pass us, he glances at me. "What?"

"Nothing," I say, with what I hope is a nonchalant shrug.

"Yeah, that look isn't nothing," he says, continuing up the hill.

I say nothing, and when he reaches the top he parks and climbs out of the car.

I stay in my seat, so he walks around to my side and swings the door open, taking the box from my lap.

"Come on," he says, gesturing for me to follow him.

"We've got stuff to do," I argue.

He turns to me, a grin spread across his face as he walks backwards. He waves at the donut box with his free hand like he's tempting a dog with a treat. "Come on, it'll be like five minutes, and I can't drive while eating one of these. There's no harm in it."

Inexplicably, I find myself climbing out of the SUV and following him.

I didn't think it would be possible, but his smile widens. "You won't regret it."

I probably will.

I make for the picnic table, but right before I sit Rhett tugs on my sleeve. He pouts a little, the look way too endearing.

"Oh, come on. We can do better than that."

I sigh, but follow him to the railing designed to stop people falling down the hill through a tangle of native bush. He turns to the right and follows the fence line to a huge tōtara tree. Once in the shade of the tree he places a hand on the railing and swings himself over in one smooth motion, the donuts still balanced perfectly in his other hand.

He turns and looks at me expectantly.

"That fence is there to stop people going over," I say.

He rolls his eyes. "Come on, sweetheart. Live a little."

I gesture uselessly back towards the car. "But we have—"

"Yeah, and we'll get to that," he says, cutting me off. "Take five minutes to chill and then we'll go back to sorting dusty old books, okay?"

I scowl.

"The sooner you come over here, the sooner we get back to it," he says, his voice a challenge.

"Fine," I huff, and clamber over the fence. I have absolutely none of the athletic grace he showed, and stumble as I land on the other side. He steadies me with a hand on my shoulder and I stare up into his face, realising how close we are, crowded into a tiny space hidden by the low branches of the tōtara. I step away, feeling the timber railings pressing into my back. "Let's get this over with."

Rhett grins, turns and disappears into the bush. I follow him because my alternative is standing here looking and feeling like an idiot while getting eaten alive by tiny bugs.

It's not far through the bush (though I'm useless at judging distances so I actually have no idea), and it doesn't take long to get to our destination.

"Woah," I breathe as I take in the sight before me. The trees end abruptly, opening onto a sort of ledge that Rhett is already lowering himself onto, showing off that casual grace again. He dangles his feet over the edge.

"Come sit," he says, patting the ground beside him.

I edge a fraction closer but have absolutely no interest in going near the edge.

I take in the view, which is even better here than from the official lookout. The sun glitters on the ocean, the blue and gold shimmering like stars in the night sky, but better. The sea salt breeze brushes against my face.

"How did you even find this place?" I ask, still not making any moves to approach the edge.

Rhett flicks the lid off the box and waves it in my direction, attempting to lure me closer. "My best friend found it when we were kids. He was up here with his family and he snuck off. He found this place, then his mum absolutely freaked out thinking she'd lost him." He smiles, but it's tinged with nostalgia and maybe a bit of sadness.

"Ricky Hill?" I ask, trying to figure out which of his friends he seems to be closest with.

His smile drops. "Is that who people think is my best friend?" He sounds curious.

I shrug. "I have no idea."

He laughs then. "Will you come sit already?"

"No, thanks. I'm good here. Besides, we should really get back."

"Sophie," he says, dragging out my name in frustration, but there's a smile behind it. "Live a little."

"Would you stop saying that?" I say, my voice coming out snappier than I intend.

"What?" He blinks at me, startled.

"Stop telling me to live a little. I live all right. My life is fine. Just because I'm not out here dangling over the edge of a cliff and whatever else it is you do with your time, doesn't mean I'm not living. You want to hang out here with someone? Bring your friend." I stop talking, heaving several deep breaths. His constant prodding is too much. I hate people telling me I need to get out and live, that I spend too much time reading or whatever. My life is as valid as everyone else's.

Rhett slides the lid back on the box of donuts and stands. Each move is slow and deliberate.

"I can't," he says, his voice low and quiet, filled with barely restrained emotion. I can't pinpoint exactly which kind.

"I can't because he's dead." I suck in a breath. I was *not* expecting that. "And you could be too—tomorrow—and the only way you'd ever have lived is through your books. You could die tomorrow and the closest thing you'll ever have to getting that tattoo you want is writing it on some kind of ridiculous to-do list."

The words hit me like a brick to the face. I want to comfort Rhett when he's clearly in pain talking about his friend … but my own emotions are taking over and I spin away from him, starting back towards the carpark.

"I'm sorry about your friend," I whisper thickly, unable to imagine what it would be like to lose Theo, then I attempt to steady my voice. "When you're finished here I need a ride back."

"Sophie," he says, stepping towards me. I shoot him a glare over my shoulder and he freezes.

A moment later his stricken face is obscured by the trees. If we'd brought my car, I'd have been happy to leave him there.

SOPHIE BARLOW IS AN AVOIDER EXTRAORDINAIRE.

I honestly thought I had her pegged.

Quiet, a bit shy, a total book nerd, obviously. A stickler for the rules.

I did not pick her for being a master at the art of avoidance.

But it's been two days since I shoved both feet in my mouth at Dusty's lookout and we haven't even been close enough for me to apologise, despite my best efforts.

I only wanted to share the place with her because I thought she'd like it. I felt like we were sort of becoming friends. Well, I was hoping we were becoming friends and I was trying to push that along. I thought she deserved to eat a donut with a spectacular view.

I didn't intend to hassle her. I definitely didn't intend to bring up Dusty.

I should have known better. I should have known that I can't function properly when Dusty is on my mind, and he's always on my mind when I'm in that spot.

Well, I'll know for next time.

I was a complete and total jerk, and I know it. I tried to apologise the whole way back to the warehouse, every time we stopped at a collection point and loaded more boxes of books into the back of the car.

The only time she spoke to me was to tell me where the next pick-up place was.

When we arrived back at the warehouse she unloaded the car box by box, avoiding even looking in my direction as I relayed with her.

I thought there were a lot of books there before, but we added another twelve boxes.

As I set down the last one, I looked around for Sophie, hoping to catch her and apologise some more, but she'd disappeared. I only saw her once more that day, tucked in a corner with a laptop across her knees. I was about to go and make a last-ditch attempt to speak to her again, to get her to speak to me again, when Grandma found me and said she was ready to leave.

I glanced back at Sophie to find her gaze locked on me. I lifted my hand, waved and sent her an apologetic smile. She scowled and went back to the screen in front of her.

It felt like a punch in the gut.

Yesterday I looked for her at school.

Things went from her not being on my radar at all, to me not being able to go anywhere without seeing her, and back to me questioning her very existence.

I saw Theo at lunchtime, walking with a group of people, but there was no sign of Sophie.

I kept waiting for her to appear as I sat with my friends, staring at the spot she'd sat under the tree the day before. But the bell for class rang and Sophie didn't show.

Today it's halfway through the lunch period when I realise she isn't going to appear, but I know where I can find her.

I need to go back to the library anyway, to see if the next book in my series is in.

I stand abruptly from the table and nearly knock Brad off the end of the bench we're squashed onto.

"You right, mate?" he asks as I swung my bag over my shoulder.

"Yeah, sorry. Just remembered I gotta go do something. Catch you later." I give the group a half-hearted wave and spin on my heel.

As I approach the glass doors of the library I see her sitting at the checkout desk, her blonde hair pulled back from her face with a headband, the little sparkly gems on it glittering every time she moves her head.

Someone approaches her, a younger student I don't know, and she greets them with a smile, chatting easily as she scans their books.

I step through the doors right as she's tucking the student's receipt into the book on top of their stack.

"Happy reading," she says to the student, who hugs the books to their chest as they leave the library.

Her gaze follows them, then adjusts slightly as she notices me, standing hesitantly beside the door.

For a split second I think she's happy to see me. The expression on her face seems to open slightly, then it slams shut, a frown creasing her features.

I step towards her, and she can't hold my gaze. She shuffles some papers on the desk, adjusts a pile of books next to her.

Resting my palm against the desk she's perched behind I lean down to speak quietly to her. "Hey. I've been looking for you."

She sighs. "What do you want?" Her tone is so … I don't even know. Like she's totally done with me.

I falter. I wanted to apologise; I wanted to make it right. But faced with her total apathy the words dry up in my throat.

She waits, fiddling with the corner of a book while I stand there trying to make my voice work again so I can explain. She raises an eyebrow. "Look, if you don't mind, I've got people to help."

I glance around and realise someone is waiting behind me. My timing, as usual, is far from impeccable. It couldn't even pass as fine. "Uh, I wanted to see if the next book I'm after is in."

She lets out a breath. "You know where it'll be if it is," she says in that same flat tone.

"Ah, yeah, right," I say and shuffle a few steps backwards. "Um, sorry. For bothering you, and for—"

"It's not back yet—*The Battle of the Labyrinth*," she says, cutting me off. "It's due though, so maybe check tomorrow."

"Oh, okay, thanks." I tap my hand against the desk a couple of times. "Right, well, I'll see you later, I guess?"

"Yeah, sure," she says, dismissing me with a turn of her head and shooting a smile at the person waiting behind me, like she doesn't care at all. Not that I really blame her.

I take a few steps towards the door and glance back at her. She tucks some stray hair behind her ear and then points towards a section of the library, obviously giving directions.

It's in that moment that I realise I never told Sophie what book I was looking for. She just somehow knows what it is.

12 /
sophie

THE FINAL BELL of the school day rings and I lower my head to rest on the desk in front of me as students spring from their seats, tossing books and pens into backpacks and racing from the room.

I relax, feeling the cool wood against my cheek and wishing I could just stay here.

"Okay, I know you like school and all, but it's still not like you to not be rushing out of here to go play with books," Theo says, nudging my leg with their foot.

I groan. I don't want to go today. I don't want to see Rhett again after that weird interaction in the library where I think I told him I knew which book he was looking for, like I was some kind of creepy stalker who looked up his borrowing history. I haven't. I just know that's what he was looking for on Monday morning.

"Come on," Theo says, picking up my backpack and tugging me from my seat. "What's up?"

I shoulder my bag as they hold it out for me, and as we start walking towards the carpark I try to figure out how to get out of this conversation. I don't want to talk about Rhett any more than I want to see him.

Theo shoulder bumps me. "Speak. You know I won't give up until you do."

That sparks a smile, because it's true.

"I don't even know," I say as we step outside the building and head in the direction of the carpark. I sigh and run my fingers through the ends of my hair, then readjust my headband.

I look up as we pass a group of people and my gaze lands squarely on Rhett. He gives me a half-hearted smile, like he's unsure of what my reaction will be. I scowl and his face falls.

"Woah, brutal, Soph," Theo mutters next to me. "I thought you guys would be the best of friends by now, or at least you wouldn't be scowling at him."

I turn away from Rhett and stomp the rest of the way to my car, tossing my bag into the back seat and slamming the door before turning to face Theo again. "Well, we're not. He's a jerk, Theo."

"He's really not," they say, studying me closely. They take me by the elbow and lead me to a bench nearby, pulling me down to sit beside them. "What happened?"

I make a growling sound, and it almost makes me laugh because I have no idea where the noise came from.

"Soph," Theo says, staring me down.

"All right. Well ... It was sort of okay. We were picking up books together on Tuesday—"

"Oh, that makes sense," Theo interrupts.

"What makes sense?"

"That whatever it was happened on Tuesday, because you've been cranky pants since then. So the timing checks out."

I roll my eyes. I haven't been cranky. Theo makes a rolling gesture with their hands, as if to say get on with it.

"Anyway, it was fine, we were maybe being friends. We were

getting along, anyway. He bought us donuts then drove us up to the lookout."

At the word "lookout" Theo's face changes, shock crossing their features. I realise that for a lot of people the lookout is a make out spot. "No, no, no. Not like that," I say. "He wasn't being sleazy."

Theo shakes their head, an odd expression still on their face, but gestures again for me to continue.

"He went over the fence and along this little path right out to the edge," I say, shuddering a little at the memory of so blatantly breaking the rules. "The view was amazing, but he kept wanting me to go near the edge, and we really needed to get back and finish picking up the books. He kept going on about how I need to 'live a little'." I emphasise the words with air quotes. "I got mad, he got mad." My voice breaks on the last word and my eyes burn as I replay the words Rhett said to me. I take a deep, shuddering breath and continue. "He told me I could be dead tomorrow and I'll never have lived except through books," I say in a rush. I squish my eyes shut, like I can avoid the pain the words caused and keep causing me.

Probably the worst part is that he's not wrong.

I mean, I'm happy with my life. I like it.

But there are definitely things I want to do … but I simply don't have the courage.

"Oh, Soph," Theo says softly as they wrap their arms around me. "There's a lot going on here."

"He told me his best friend died," I murmur into Theo's shoulder, the tears welling properly now.

"Yeah, he did," Theo says.

I pull back from the hug, trying to decipher the tone I heard in their voice. They look so sad, even though I'm the one crying.

"You know my cousin Dustin? Who died last year?"

I nod. It had been awful. Someone our age dying from cancer. I didn't know Dustin directly, but I know how much his death had affected Theo.

"He was Rhett's best friend. That place ... that place was Dusty's. The fact that Rhett took you there ... I imagine that was a pretty big deal for him. But," Theo says, holding up a hand to forestall anything I might have been about to say, "that doesn't excuse what he said. Or more, the way he said it."

"What do you mean, 'the way he said it'?" I ask, because it sounds suspiciously like Theo is taking Rhett's side.

"Look, Soph." Theo exhales a heavy sigh. "He's not exactly wrong about the living a little."

I flinch.

"I know, I know," Theo says. "Look, I get being scared. Trust me, I get it. More than most. But you can't let it control your entire life. You can't let that fear take over everything."

"But I'm not scared. I like my life. I'm living." I try to convince myself as much as I'm trying to convince Theo.

"Yeah, but not fully. There're things you want to do. I know there are. I've seen your list." They give me a look at my gasp of indignation. "You're not that sneaky with it." Another long pause, as though Theo is trying to decide if they should say more. "This is probably outside of, like, my friendship boundaries or whatever, but your mum ... she kind of keeps you close."

"Yeah," I snap. "That's what parents are supposed to do; look after us." Theo is way too close to the painful truth. This whole conversation is pressing on sore spots I'd rather pretend didn't exist.

I don't want to think about my list of really stupid things I want to do one day. None of it is outrageous. It's basic things most teenagers wouldn't think twice about, but ... for me they feel momentous, huge, overwhelming. I sigh and tune back into what Theo is saying.

"Mmm, yeah, to a point. But you're almost eighteen. She doesn't let you go to parties, or stay over at a friend's house unless she's done a thorough background check on the family. She didn't even let you go on that school trip."

"The school trip that was several days in the bush with no contact with the outside world? I didn't even want to go on it. Just like I don't want to go to parties," I say, emotion making my voice rise.

Theo shrugs. "I don't know, Soph. I think I messed this up. I'm sorry. But the main point you should take away from this, is that Rhett isn't a bad guy. He's actually pretty great. He's worth being friends with. I promise you."

13 /
rhett

I'M PRETTY sure Sophie is crying on Theo's shoulder across the carpark right now, and it's twisting me up inside.

I really hope I'm not the cause of her upset.

Ricky says my name like it's not the first time.

"What?" I say, tuning back into the conversation happening around me.

"I asked if you were coming down to the beach?"

"The beach?" I've really not being paying attention to this conversation at all.

"Yeah, the beach. Big sandy thing on the edge of the ocean. A bunch of us are going down there this afternoon."

"Oh, nah, I can't man, sorry."

"Have you got a girlfriend you haven't told us about yet?" Ricky asks, while Brad and Evan hoot with laughter in the background like it's the most hilarious thing anyone's ever said.

I scowl. "No," I mutter. "I'm just busy."

"Yeah, you're never around anymore," Evan says. "My money's on a girl."

I roll my eyes. I could tell them the truth, that I'm effectively grounded and being forced to spend my afternoons sorting dusty books for charity.

The thing is, I don't actually mind it that much, and I really can't be bothered dealing with their opinions or their suggestions about how to get out of it.

I don't actually want to get out of it, I realise.

I glance across the carpark again. Sophie and Theo are still talking, but it doesn't look like anyone's crying anymore. The tightness in my chest releases a little. Theo stands, offers a hand to Sophie and she takes it, allowing herself to be pulled to standing. Theo gives Sophie a sort of half hug, boops her on the nose and spins away, jogging across the carpark to where their younger brother is waiting.

Sophie watches Theo go, then glances in my direction. I quickly avert my eyes but I'm pretty sure she caught me looking. By the time I look back, Sophie is in her car.

"I'd better go," I say to Ricky, Evan and Brad, turning away from them before they have a chance to rib me more about my fictional girlfriend. "Catch you tomorrow," I call over my shoulder as I head for my car.

Safely ensconced inside, I wrack my brain for a way to make things right with Sophie. I've been trying to come up with something ever since those hideous words left my mouth.

An idea sparks in my mind. It's not much, but it's a start.

AS EXPECTED, Sophie is at the book warehouse before I arrive. She's tucked away in the corner, mostly hidden behind a stack of books.

I wave across the room to Grandma but I don't go and say hello yet. I have a delivery to make first. I take a deep breath and stride across the huge space. More tables are being pulled out and set up as we sort more books, so there's a few obstacles I have to skirt around—including Trevor, who's eyeing the box in my hand with a gleam in his eye. I avoid eye contact and keep going, heading directly for Sophie.

As I approach her, my steps slow of their own accord.

She hasn't looked up yet and now I can see what she's doing— scribbling notes furiously on a sheet of paper.

I clear my throat, stopping a short distance away from her.

She glances up, gasps and clutches a hand to her chest. It's obvious I startled her.

"Uh, I'm sorry," I say. "I didn't mean to give you a fright."

She keeps staring at me, her eyes open wide, and takes a few breaths. She doesn't say anything.

"I, um, I brought you these." I hold out the box, and when she doesn't reach for it I slide it onto the table between us.

She blinks at the box, then back at me. She pushes her glasses up her nose. "You brought me two-day old donuts?"

"No. I ate those donuts. These are new ones, because you didn't get to try the other ones."

"Because you ate them?"

"Ah … yes?" I don't know why I say it like a question. I don't know where this conversation is going. I'm a little startled she even responded when I spoke to her.

Sophie's lip twitches. Is she going to smile? Maybe she was, but not anymore. Her mouth returns to its usual position. She sighs and fiddles with the pen in her hand. It's sparkly and purple and has an actual feather sticking out the top of it. It's ridiculous, and also so incredibly Sophie I can't help but like it.

"I—I wanted to apologise," I say, after another beat of silence passes between us. "About the other day. About what I said." My throat goes dry, and the rest of the words get stuck.

She waits, staring me down while she taps the pen against her paper. "You know that's not actually an apology, don't you?"

What the hell? She's busting my behind while I'm in the middle of my apology speech?

"Well, I haven't got to that part yet," I say, my voice sounding scratchy. "I wasn't done." I scowl at her and the corner of her mouth twitches again.

"Oh, excuse me then. You may continue," she says, gesturing with a "go on" movement of her hand.

"I'm sorry," I say. "I'm sorry for what I said. It was totally out of line and I shouldn't have said it. I'm sorry."

She stares up at me for another moment and I wonder if three sorrys is enough or if I should throw another couple out there for good measure.

Abruptly she stands. "You didn't say what you said was wrong, though."

"What do you mean?"

"I mean, you said you shouldn't have said it. But you didn't say what you said was wrong or incorrect in any way."

I feel like I'm walking into a trap. It's that feeling when you're watching an action movie and you know something is going to happen, but you can't do anything except wait for the jump scare.

"Uh…" I don't know what to say that's not going to make this conversation go south again. I don't even know her well enough to judge her on whether she's living her life fully or not. I'm opening my mouth to say tell her exactly that when she speaks again.

"Apparently, you're not the only one who thinks so. And I have it on good authority that you're not a bad guy."

I blink at her. This is not going how I expected. I wonder who her good authority on me is. I assume it's Theo. I hope it's Theo. I hope they have a good opinion of me, though I'm not sure how good of an opinion "not a bad guy" actually is. It's not a ringing endorsement. I'm still trying to process where this is going when Sophie steps around the table and continues talking.

"Because of that, I want you to help me with something."

"Help you with something?"

She nods and holds out the crumpled paper in her hand.

I take it and stare down at the sheet that's clearly been folded and unfolded multiple times, tucked into pockets and shoved into backpacks.

It's her list.

The To Do List.

14 /
sophie

RHETT IS STARING down at my list and immediately I regret everything.

I shouldn't have shown him this. I shouldn't have handed it over. My brain scrambles for a way to get out of what I've started.

Eventually, after what feels like three years of Rhett's eyes scanning down the page, he lifts his gaze to meet mine.

"What is this?" he asks, his brows drawn down in a frown.

"It's a list," I say, stepping closer and reaching out for the paper. "Don't worry about it. It was a dumb idea." As my fingertips skim the edge of the sheet Rhett jerks it away, holding it high enough that I can't reach it. I stretch on my tiptoes, but he's got it just out of reach. He glances back and forth from the list to me.

"And you what? Want me to help you check things off it?" he asks, as though I haven't spoken.

I stop reaching for the paper. There's no way I'm getting it back until he's ready to give it to me, unless I jump. I consider it for a second, but I feel like a big enough fool right now. I don't need to add to that.

I heave out a breath. "Yes."

He takes a step back, bringing the paper down so he can study it again. I realise how close I've been to him in my attempts to get the paper back and I hurriedly step backwards.

There's nothing I can do except stand here and watch as his eyes roam over the page then settle on me again.

"Sweetheart," he says, his voice low, and although I want to hiss and scowl at him for calling me such a ridiculous endearment, I realise I've missed him calling me that. My eyes lock on his and he continues, "You want me to take you skinny dipping?" He raises an eyebrow and my face catches fire.

I may as well spontaneously combust right here and now. Burn into a little pile of ashes on the ground.

"No," I snap, reaching out for the paper again. "It says 'spontaneous swimming'; that's not the same thing."

His mouth curves into a smug little grin and I want to wipe it off his face. Something glints in his eyes—humour, challenge, maybe proof that he's really a jerk and Theo was way, way wrong.

Rhett is looking me up and down like he's undressing me with his eyes, probably working out if I'm worth going skinny dipping with. Which is *not* on the list.

"Bowling, dye your hair, stay out all night …" He runs down the list. His other eyebrow joins the first and he focusses on me again. "A perfect first kiss under the stars."

I didn't think it was possible, but my face burns even hotter. Why didn't I think to rewrite the list into a version that was suitable for someone else to see? I should have taken half the things off it. I shouldn't have given it to Rhett at all.

"You want me to help you with this list?"

I'm committed now. I was committed the second I handed over that sheet of paper.

"Yes," I say, my voice coming out weak and breathy. I clear my throat and say again, "Yes. You're going to help me."

"And here I was thinking you were asking for my help, not

demanding it," he says, that mirth or challenge or whatever in his eye sparking again.

"You're going to help me or I'll tell your grandma you're not pulling your weight around here. That you won't help me on pick-ups and you're generally being a jerk."

He blinks at me, then lets out a soft laugh. "Sweetheart, are you *blackmailing me*?"

Uh, am I? I guess I probably am. I force myself to stand straighter, even though all I want to do is slink back behind the table and bury myself under a stack of books.

"Yes," I say, forcing conviction into my voice. "You're the one who pointed out I need to 'live a little'." I form air quotes with my fingers. "So you're going to help me do it."

"And how do you know my grandma even cares what I do here?"

"Because you're clearly not here by choice. You've already asked me what I'm in for, and you nearly fell over when you realised I'm here of my own free will. This is obviously some kind of punishment for you."

He tilts his head slightly, studies me carefully then flicks his eyes over the paper again.

"I can't help you with all of it," he says. "But I could help you with some."

"Good. Thank you." I turn away, heading for my pile of books before my confidence falls and shatters at my feet. I spin back. "Also, if you tell a single person about the list or anything on it … well, you know," I say, pointedly glancing across the warehouse at his grandma.

"Noted," he says, then drags a chair over and falls into it across the table from me. "Now, donut?"

I roll my eyes as he lifts the lid of the Oh, Sweet Bagels box he carried in with him and slides it toward me. I glance in, not sure what I'm expecting, but it isn't a replica of the box I chose on Tuesday.

I spin it around so the boysenberry custard donut is closest to him. "That's yours, isn't it?"

"Sweetheart, they're apology donuts. You get them all."

"Apology donuts?"

"Yeah, remember how I came over here and told you how sorry I was for being a total jerk? They're here to back me up." He runs a hand through his hair as he thinks. "Or maybe they're the real apology and you don't care a bit about the actual apology."

I can't help it. I laugh.

"You have it," he says, spinning the box back to me. "Watching you eat my favourite donut ever will be good punishment. Serves me right for being an idiot."

I reach into the box and take it, watching him closely as I do, almost daring him to fight me for it. He stares right back at me as I bring it to my mouth and take a bite. He's right. It's amazing.

He grins. "Besides, I've got one for myself right here," he says as he slides a bag I haven't noticed out from behind the box. He pulls out the same flavour donut and takes a huge bite.

"You're utterly ridiculous," I say, then we both burst out laughing—as much as you can when your mouth is full of the most delicious food to ever exist.

SOPHIE BARLOW BLACKMAILED ME.

She stood right in front of me and blackmailed me into helping her with this list of hers.

I didn't tell her there was no need to threaten me. I'd have done it anyway, but I did really enjoy those few moments when I got a rise out of her.

I kind of loved the way she stood her ground and glared at me while threatening to tell Grandma I was being a useless jerk.

Got to give her credit for that.

What I don't get though, is why the girl who did that needs me to help her check things off this list. Why does she need me to help her go to an arcade? Or dye her hair? Or do any of the other things on the list?

I sure as heck don't know how she expects me to help her achieve her perfect first kiss under a starry night sky. I'm pretty sure the kiss has to mean something and can't just be making out with me for the sake of ticking something off. I feel like even suggesting that is going to get me a punch to the face … or worse. But how I'm supposed to help with that one, I don't know.

I sigh and roll over on my bed. It's been a couple of hours

since we got home from book sorting. I sat through dinner with my grandparents and escaped to my room under the excuse of homework, but I haven't been able to think about English at all. Not with Sophie's list burning a hole in my pocket.

She's written her phone number across the bottom of the page in her swirly handwriting. Seeing it there does something funny to my chest. There's an odd feeling in there, like something is trapped behind my ribs.

I sit bolt upright.

Am I into Sophie?

I snort and flop back onto my back. Nah, there's no way. It's a shadow feeling, because it's been so long since I've spent any time with a girl.

It wouldn't matter anyway, because I'm pretty sure messed up jerks on grandparent-imposed probation are not Sophie's type.

I type her number into my phone and add her as a contact. My thumbs hover over the keyboard deliberating over her name. Capital S … I know I should save her as Sophie, but I don't. I type a word, follow it with a sunshine emoji and hit save.

I study the list again, wondering where to start, what I can do to help her and why she even thinks she needs my help.

She's drawn little flowers down the edges of the paper and coloured them in pink, blue and purple. Each item on the list is marked by another flower, a simple five-petalled daisy. The whole thing screams Sophie—until I look at the items listed.

I pick up my phone again, open a new text message and add her name.

RHETT:

Are you free tomorrow after school?

I wait.

And wait.

I glance at the screen of my phone every minute to see if I've somehow missed her reply. Of course, I haven't.

After ten minutes of paranoia I shove myself off the bed. I want to pace. I don't know why I'm so agitated about her texting me back.

Then I realise why she might not text me back.

RHETT:

This is Rhett btw

What an idiot.

I fall into my desk chair and check the silence switch on my phone isn't turned on. As if I haven't done that a billion times in the last ten minutes.

I toss my phone onto my desk and open my laptop, reaching into my school bag for a text book. I've got to do something to try to distract my brain. I get the feeling my grandparents aren't going to be down with me heading out at this time of night, which is what I used to do before the last strands of my life holding everything together snapped.

I let my head fall forward and catch it in my hands, resting my elbows on the desk. I'm about to spiral. I know it. I'm about to fall down the twisting vortex of a black hole that are my thoughts, my agony, my grief.

The pain of losing my best friend never really goes away. It's always there, lingering right on the edge, and most of the time it's avoidable. I wouldn't say it's easy to ignore, but I can push it aside and carry on with life.

I think it helps that we didn't go to the same school. As much as he was a part of my daily life, I didn't see him every day at school. While I'm there I can pretend that he's going about his day across town.

But it's in the quiet moments that the memories overwhelm

me and the devastation takes hold again.

I used to go out and drive when these feelings claimed me. I'd drive up to the lookout and sit in Dusty's favourite spot or I'd lie in the middle of the soccer field where we'd first become friends, playing on the same team when we were kids. Occasionally I'd go to the beach and scream at the ocean, letting it all out as the sound of waves crashing against the sand drowned out the agony.

But I can't go out anymore. Not since I screwed up so badly. There's no way Grandad will let me walk out of here.

There's no way I can study now though, so I shove my textbook back into my bag. Somewhere along the line I'm going to have to catch up on all this work I'm avoiding if I want to do more than barely scrape by in my final exams.

But tonight is not the night for it. I head for the bathroom, brush my teeth and get ready for bed. I've learnt that sometimes the best way to avoid the pain is to sleep through it.

By the time I'm back in the floral travesty that is my new bedroom, there's a message on my phone. I grin when I see the name.

SWEETHEART:

Hey Rhett. I was going to sort more books. Do you not have to tomorrow?

I fall into bed, hit reply and tell Sophie my plan.

16 /
sophie

I **FIDGET** as I wait by the edge of the student carpark. I mess with my hair and adjust the straps of my backpack, and I can't decide if I should lean against the fence or stand here awkwardly and wait.

Half of the school has emptied but Rhett is nowhere in sight, and I wonder if he's set me up as some kind of weird and mean joke. He's got way better ammunition to use against me though, so I'm pretty sure he hasn't stood me up.

I was surprised when he texted me last night, even though I'd written my number on the list I gave him and he said he would be in touch.

I was even more surprised when he asked if I could get a ride to school so we could leave together and check off our first item.

That's what he said.

Our first item.

Like we're a team.

That one little word made me embarrassingly happy.

He wouldn't tell me what we're doing today though, so I hope my usual jeans and sweatshirt combo is appropriate. I wore my favourite one today. It's slouchy and cosy and dark purple with white hearts printed across the front.

"You sure you don't need a ride?" Theo asks, arriving at my side.

"Do you ever say hello to anyone?" I respond.

They roll their eyes and laugh. "Yes. Just not you."

"I'm not sure if I should be offended or not."

"Definitely not," Theo says, giving my hand a squeeze. "It's because you're special. Now, do you need a ride?"

"No, I told you, Rhett's giving me one."

"What's going on?" Theo narrows their eyes at me like I'm acting suspiciously, which maybe I am.

I haven't exactly told them what I'm doing—that Rhett is helping me with the list.

"Nothing is going on," I say, hoping my voice remains steady and the eye contact I'm forcing myself to hold isn't too intense. "He's giving me a ride today. That's it."

Theo studies me and I force myself not to look away or fidget. They open their mouth to speak.

"Heya, sweetheart," Rhett says behind me, and I breathe a sigh of relief.

I don't know why I'm reluctant to tell Theo about the list, or more importantly, Rhett's involvement in the list. But I don't think I want anyone to know. It's hugely embarrassing.

I turn to Rhett and he's grinning down at me. I scowl at his ridiculous nickname for me. He always says it with exactly the right amount of challenge and humour so I know it isn't an endearment, but I can also tell he's not being cruel when he says it. I don't know how the name has stuck but I get the feeling that arguing is not going to help my case.

I totally, one hundred percent ignore the little thrill of something that races through me every time he says it.

"Hey," I mutter.

"And good afternoon, Theo," Rhett says.

"Rhett," Theo says, their scrutiny now trained on him. "What are you two doing this afternoon?"

Rhett shrugs. "Nothing much. Going to drool over books. Well, I won't be. This one will be." He reaches out and ruffles my hair. I swat his hand away and his grin stretches wider. "You ready to go?"

"Yup," I say. "Catch you later." I wave to Theo and follow Rhett to his car. "Did you lie to my best friend about what we're doing today?" I'm trying not to feel guilty by default. I didn't lie... I just didn't tell the truth.

Rhett slides into the car and shoves his backpack between the front seats into the back. I put mine on the backseat using the door, then climb into the front. "I wasn't sure if you wanted me to tell the truth or not ... but if it makes you feel better, I can give you a book to drool over so we won't be lying at all."

"Oh." Well, that was oddly thoughtful. I twist around in my seat to reach my backpack. "That reminds me." I rummage around, and after a moment locate what I'm looking for. I turn back to the front, resting the book in my lap. "I checked this out for you today."

Rhett glances at the book as he waits for the car in front of us to pull out of the carpark. Then he does a double take.

"How did you know?" he asks.

I shrug, heat finding my cheeks. "I returned the third book and was shelving it when I found you in the same section, annoyed that the fourth book wasn't there. I put two and two together."

I mean, I probably wouldn't have paid any attention to these details usually, but for some reason they stuck in my mind. Because it was Rhett.

"Anyway," I say after a moment of him not saying anything. "I had to get it out in my name, so please return it on time, but I saw it come in and didn't want someone else to check it out before you got to it."

We stop at another intersection and Rhett looks over at me, a soft smile on his face. There's a look in his eyes that I can't decipher, but it feels significant.

"Thank you. I'll take good care of it."

He lifts his hand from where it's resting on the gear stick and it hovers in the air between us for a long moment. I feel my breath catch as his fingers stray towards me. Then he lowers his hand again, putting it back on the gear stick as he clears his throat and returns his focus to the road as the traffic begins to move.

We fall into silence. The radio is playing a pop song I don't know and I'm at a loss for what to say. I don't know why but this moment feels emotionally charged, and I'm not great with emotionally charged moments.

Eventually we approach the turn off for the book warehouse, and Rhett breaks the increasingly awkward silence. It didn't start awkward, but the longer it went on the worse it got.

"Do you need to do anything at the warehouse today?"

"No. I only turn up when I want to. I told Tonya I wouldn't be there today. Do you need to be there, though?"

"Nah," he says. "My sentence is Monday to Thursday and an as-yet-undisclosed amount of time on the weekend. I'm hoping it'll be reduced for good behaviour." He shoots me a grin, but it looks a little strained.

"So, what's the plan then?" I ask.

Rhett's grin relaxes. "Well, I thought we'd go have some fun. Sound good, sweetheart?"

rhett

AS I DRIVE I can't help glancing at the book in Sophie's lap.

She went to the trouble of checking it out for me, in her name. I'm not sure which is tripping me out more: the fact that she thought of me enough to figure out the book I wanted and to check it out before anyone else could, or that she's trusting me with a book under her name. She's putting her library reputation in my hands.

I think it's the trust thing. It's definitely the trust thing.

She groans and drops her head back against the headrest when I call her sweetheart, and I laugh.

"Why do you call me that?" she asks.

"Because every time I do you pull that face."

She groans again and glares at me.

"Yep, that one."

"Will me telling you to stop have any effect?"

"Not at all, sweetheart." I grin, and her face scrunches into that disgruntled expression again.

I let the conversation drop as I concentrate on turning into the carpark of our destination and finding a free space. As I pull into one and park the car, I turn to face her.

"Look, I started it because I'm a jerk, and I continued it because it was fun and I didn't think you minded that much. Yeah, I know it annoys you, but I didn't really think it was a problem. If it is, I'll stop."

She watches me from behind her glasses, then pushes them up her nose. I'm beginning to wonder if she does that when she's nervous. "You'd stop if I asked you to?"

"Yeah, of course. I'm not doing it to be a jerk. Not anymore, anyway. You kind of caught me in a bad mood that day we met."

"Ha. I hadn't noticed," she says. She tries to smother it, but a laugh escapes.

"Oh, shut up," I say, laughing along with her. "You ready to go check off your first list item?"

She nods and climbs out of the car, and we head for the entrance to the building.

"So you've never been to an arcade?"

Sophie's cheeks immediately flush pink. "Um, no. That's why it's on the list."

"You've never gone with Theo?"

"I've never gone with anyone. I just said that."

"No." I lift my hands up in a "hold on" gesture. "I mean, why don't you go with Theo?"

Sophie looks at me, puzzled, then shrugs.

"Theo is epic in an arcade. High scores everywhere. Beats everyone. It's ridiculous."

"How …" Sophie starts then trails off, looking even more confused than she did a moment ago. "How do you know this about my best friend and I don't?"

"Because Theo's cousin is my best friend. Was." The pang of loss hits again like it always does when I have to figure out if Dusty is still my best friend, even when he's been gone a year. I shake the feeling off as best I can, but it lingers. "Dusty was huge into video games. We went to arcades all the time. Most of his birthday parties when we were kids were at arcades. That's where I first met Theo. They were making this guy cry over air hockey."

"I didn't know you and Theo knew each other until this week," she says.

"Yeah, it's … it's kind of weird. We'd hang out with Dusty, but never apart. And now that he's gone …" I trail off and shrug, trying to shake off that loss again. I should know better. It's not going anywhere.

"You've lost that thing you had in common?" Sophie asks, and I feel a light touch on my arm. I glance down and she's resting her fingertips against my sleeve. I shiver as she brushes the fabric. Then she gives a gentle squeeze around my wrist and lets go. "You've got something else in common again now … if you want to hang out with Theo, I mean." Sophie adjusts her glasses. It's definitely a nervous gesture.

"Yeah, I guess we do," I say, smiling down at her. "Sometimes it's easier to avoid the reminders though, so I get it if Theo doesn't want to see me. I don't know how much losing Dusty affected them."

Sophie grabs hold of my sleeve again and tugs me to the side, right as I was about to step through the door into the indoor complex that includes a bowling alley, mini golf, trampoline park and the reason we're here: the arcade. She pulls me over to the side of the building and stops me with her hand encircling my wrist again. I can feel a fingertip brushing the skin of my palm.

"I don't really know, to be honest. Theo didn't talk about it too much, but maybe they would with you. If you wanted to. But Theo likes you. They told me you're one of the good guys."

"So that's why you accepted my apology?"

She blushes. "Pretty much, yeah."

"But you didn't tell Theo about the list?"

Her cheeks turn an even darker shade of pink. "Theo knows about the list. They don't know everything that's on it, or about your involvement. I'd, uh, appreciate if you didn't tell them that part."

"It's all good, sweetheart," I say, hoping that me using her nickname won't break whatever this is turning into. I told her I'd stop if she asked me to, and she didn't. Her brow scrunches a fraction, but I also notice her lip twitching, like she wants to smile. I'm in the clear. "I won't say a word to anyone. Wouldn't want you to dob me in to my grandma." I wrap my arm around her shoulders in a friendly gesture. There is absolutely nothing more to it than that. "Now, come on, I'll teach you everything I know so next time you can bring Theo and hustle them with all your epic arcade skills."

"All right, bring it on," she says, not shrugging off my arm as I lead her through the doorway into the neon-lit arcade.

18 /
sophie

I AM SO SHOCKINGLY bad at air hockey, Rhett ends up laughing so hard he has to sit down. On the floor.

By the time I leave my end of the table and reach him, he's wiping tears from his eyes and barely getting his breathing back under control.

Unfortunately, not only was I really, really bad at air hockey, I went into the game with so much confidence, and my stupid, usually dormant competitive streak came out to play. Like, how hard could it be?

Then Rhett beat me in about five seconds flat. Both times. Even when he went easy on me the second time. He didn't tell me he'd gone easy on me, but I could tell. And I still sucked so much I was quite ready to crawl into a hole and pretend I'd never met Rhett Carmichael.

Instead I find myself staring down at him as he sits on the arcade floor, wheezing.

Eventually he climbs to his feet and faces me.

My cheeks are burning. This is why I hate trying new things. I'm so terribly bad at them. I don't even know how to talk to Rhett after this total disaster.

"Okay, so the air hockey needs some work," he says, then slings his arm across my shoulders and spins me around. "That bouncy ball thing or racing next?"

I groan. "Neither. Is there a third option? Like leaving?"

The arcade is busy, filled with over-excited rowdy kids and flashing lights that are giving me a headache. Or maybe it's the anxiety of being in such a crowded, chaotic space that's giving me a headache.

I wasn't entirely truthful with Rhett when we arrived. Because I *have* been to an arcade before, when I was much younger. All I remember is the noise and the over-bright, colourful lights, and the crushing weight of panic on my chest when I lost track of my mum for what felt like hours, but was in reality only a few minutes.

It's why I've never come back, even when Theo invited me. Not that I would have been allowed.

It's also why I'm relieved Rhett didn't mention what we were doing today ahead of time. If he had, I would have spent my day on edge about whether I'd be able to walk through the doors. It definitely helped having that conversation about Rhett's friend when we arrived. Being able to offer him some kind of comfort helped distract me from what I was stepping into.

After I adjusted to the wall of sound, Rhett dragged me from game to game, explaining how each of them worked and forcing me to play his favourites.

I'm not any better at them than I am at air hockey, but Rhett seems to think I need to keep on playing in case I've magically improved in the last half hour.

He uses his arm around my shoulders to turn me a little to the right, so I'm looking directly at the food counter. "This would be option three," he says, breath warm against my hair.

"Option three for sure," I say.

He tsks. "You won't get better if you don't practise."

"I don't think I need to get better. I only wanted to try it, not become master of the arcade," I say as we step up to the counter. We order loaded fries and milkshakes then head for an empty table in the back corner of the room.

Rhett leaves his arm across my shoulders until we reach the booth and we slide into opposite sides. As usual with Rhett, I'm not sure what to make of his casual affection.

When he first slung his arm around my shoulders outside the building I almost tripped over my own feet in surprise. As we played various games he touched me in the most casual way, adjusting my grip on the ball I was trying to throw through the hoop or nudging me to stand closer to a game, his hand covering mine as I tried to manoeuvre one of those stupid crane machines.

Every time my heart trips a little, and I have to remind myself they aren't flirty touches. They're way too casual for that.

Not that I have any experience with flirty touches, so how would I know the difference?

But I'm ninety-nine percent certain that's not his intention, so I am definitely *not* going to think he's flirting then develop a huge, embarrassing crush on him. There's no way.

"Guess I won't be hustling Theo anytime soon, huh?" I say before we can fall into an awkward silence.

Rhett laughs, shakes his head and buries his face in his hands for a few seconds before facing me again, comical despair sketched across his features. "You're not allowed to tell anyone that I taught you things. I can't have your arcade incompetence tarnishing my reputation."

I snort. "Trust me, I won't be telling anyone about this experience. Ever."

A look I can't decipher crosses Rhett's face, but he doesn't have a chance to reply. Our buzzer goes off telling us our food is ready, and he springs up, heading to the counter to collect it before I've gathered my wits enough to realise what the noise is.

He sets the tray on the table, falls into his seat with that ridiculous casual ease he's constantly showing off and throws a fry into his mouth.

"Ah!" he gasps, then points to the plate. "Really hot." He pants like a dog then takes a pull of his milkshake. I laugh. "I love how concerned for my welfare you are," he says.

I take a sip of my own milkshake and shrug.

He shakes his head. "Okay, so, while you are not … umm … great at the arcade thing, you have officially been to one, so we can check that off the list."

I agree and take a fry off the plate, blowing on it before checking to see if it's an acceptable temperature. Rhett's super mature about me mocking him and pokes his tongue out at me.

"So," he says. "I can help you with most of it, probably, but there're a couple of things I can't."

"Oh? What ones?" I try to remember what's on the list, which should be easier than it is, considering I wrote it.

"I can't get you a tattoo. You'll need adult permission for that, and even though I'm eighteen, I'm not taking on your mum over that."

"Okay, that's fair," I agree. "Even once I'm eighteen I don't know how I'll get that one past her."

"I also can't do the fireworks one, and the kiss under the stars."

It could be the weird neon glow from all the arcade lights, but I swear Rhett blushes as he says the word kiss. He also suddenly can't meet my eyes, which is very un-Rhett-like behaviour.

I swallow the weird lump that's appeared in my throat. "Ah,

um, yeah. Okay." I fiddle with my milkshake glass, drawing patterns in the condensation. It doesn't seem right that I suddenly feel bereft because Rhett doesn't want to kiss me.

I've never even considered kissing him until this moment.

Suddenly, I'd really like to know what it feels like.

I THINK I BROKE SOPHIE.

I shouldn't have mentioned the kissing item on her list.

Or maybe it was the fireworks, but I'm pretty sure the mention of fireworks wouldn't make her face turn as bright red as the tomato sauce I'm currently pouring onto the side of the plate of fries.

I have a sudden thought: she might have given me that list because of that item. Like she chose me for a reason. Then I shove the thought away, because I am totally not Sophie's type.

She'll want someone sweet and romantic and actually into books, not someone who reads the same series on repeat because he somehow believes it'll keep his best friend's memory alive. The words my ex-girlfriend said to me as she dumped me ring in my ears.

Yeah, I'm definitely not the one for Sophie.

I clear my throat and try to rescue this conversation. Things were going so well until I mentioned kissing.

"I figure you'd want it to mean something. You seem like the kind of girl who'd want that."

"What's that supposed to mean?" She finally meets my eyes again.

"Nothing bad, I promise you." The steely glint in her eyes fades. "Look," I say, reaching across the table and covering her hand with mine. "It's not a bad thing to want it to mean something, to want it to be with someone who's special. If that doesn't matter to you, then I got you, sweetheart. But I know you better than that."

She blushes even harder, but she doesn't pull away from my touch. She gives a tiny nod. "You're right," she whispers.

"It's okay," I whisper back. "It's a good thing, I promise."

"It's super dorky," she mutters, and I laugh. I can't help it, she's so damn endearing. As soon as the sound leaves my body I worry that I'm going to upset her, that she's going to think I'm laughing *at* her, but her mouth tilts up.

"Nah, it's not. Do you have someone in mind? Maybe I can help, er, move things along?" I have no idea how I would actually do that beyond approaching whoever she's crushing on and saying the very childish "My friend thinks you're cute" thing.

Sophie looks a little stunned at my question. "Erm, there's not really anyone I have in mind, no."

"Well, what's your type? I can help you narrow it down? Find you some options?"

Sophie stares across the room and I turn to see what's caught her attention. A girl and guy, probably a year or two older than us, are on the dance machine. It's clearly her idea, but he's valiantly trying to keep up while she giggles at his awkwardness. Their song ends and he catches her around the waist, laughing along with her until he presses a gentle kiss to her forehead, causing her to go still and soft in his arms, smiling up at him. As they step off the machine and disappear into the crowd, I realise I know them.

"I don't know what my type is … but them," Sophie says, her voice barely audible. "I want that."

"Jax?" I ask, turning back to Sophie. "Or Essie?"

Her eyes cut to me, then she relaxes. "Not them specifically. But yeah, um, either." Her cheeks turn pink. "She's so cool. I'd give anything to be like her. I don't know him, but when I've seen them together he's always so sweet to her. They always look like they're having fun, like they're happy." She sighs and slumps in her seat. "I don't know what I want, or why I even want it."

"It's okay to want someone to want you like that," I say, thinking over the words she used to describe Essie and Jax. Sweet, fun, happy.

"How about we go back to you not being able to help me with that one?" Sophie says, sitting up tall again and squaring her shoulders, obviously putting that conversation behind us.

I cough as I inhale my milkshake wrong. "Yeah," I say, my voice croaky and rough. "Probably for the best."

"Yeah, I think so." Sophie shoves a handful of fries into her mouth.

Time for a new topic of conversation. I wrack my brain trying to think what else was on the list.

"Rhett!"

A tiny, human-shaped missile collides with me and knocks me several inches down the booth seat. I'm glad I'm not on an actual chair.

I untangle myself from the child and set them on the seat next to me.

"Asher, my man," I say to the little boy beside me. "What are you doing here?"

"Mum brought us because Ellie won some prize thing that got us free games." Asher bounces on the seat. He's eyeing up the plate of fries. I grab a couple and hand them to him. His eyes go wide, like I've handed him a block of solid gold. Kids are so easy to please.

"Asher," his mum, Aimee, says, hurrying up to the table. "You can't run off like that." She notices me and her expression freezes for an instant, before breaking into a smile. "Hey, Rhett love, sorry for interrupting your date." She glances at Sophie and her gaze softens.

"Oh, no worries. It's not a date, we're just … learning how bad someone can be at arcade games."

Sophie huffs, but she's smiling. "Rude and uncalled for."

I grin. "Aimee, this is Sophie. Sophie, this is Aimee. Dusty's mum." My voice catches on my friend's name. "And this," I continue, clearing my throat, "is Asher." I ruffle his hair and he beams up at me.

"Hi," Sophie says. "Nice to meet you. Are you Theo's aunt, then?"

Aimee smiles at Sophie. I get the feeling all adults smile at Sophie. "Yeah, I am."

"Sophie and Theo are besties," I put in.

"Is Theo here? I want to show them how good I got at air hockey," Asher says.

"Nah, Theo isn't here this time," I say. An idea pops into my head. "Actually, Aimee, we could use your expertise."

"Oh yeah? What're you up to now?" Aimee doesn't smile at me with that soft look like she did at Sophie. The look she's giving me is trying to figure out how much trouble I'm about to cause.

"Sophie here wants to dye her hair. Perhaps you could guide us?" I glance at Sophie, who's sitting there quietly fiddling with her glass. I reach across the table again and tap her hand. "Aimee's a hairdresser."

"Oh, that's really cool," she says. "I don't think I can afford a salon, though. I was thinking I'd have to do box dye."

"Can I sit?" Aimee gestures at the spot next to Sophie, who nods and slides over to make room. "Do you have something specific in mind? Colour or anything?"

Sophie nods and shoots a glance at me, like she's nervous. Not nervous about talking to Aimee; nervous about my reaction.

"Hey, Asher, how about you show *me* how good you got at air hockey? Will I do, since Theo isn't here?" I lock eyes with Sophie as I slide out of the booth. "You good for a bit?"

She nods.

One game of air hockey later and Aimee and Sophie are ready to go.

"I'll do her hair," Aimee tells me. "Right now, free of charge, if you babysit these two." She gestures at Asher and his sister Ellie, who's shooting hoops and racking up the points. "Entertain them for the next couple of hours and feed them dinner."

I glance at Sophie standing at Aimee's shoulder, a hopeful look on her face.

"You ready to do this, sweetheart?" She nods. "All right then, looks like I'm babysitting. Let me know when you're done and I'll come pick you up."

"Thank you," she says as she rushes towards me and wraps her arms around me in a breathless hug. "For all of this," she whispers in my ear before she pulls away and disappears through the doors with Aimee, who at some point must have said goodbye to Ellie and Asher, but I don't recall it.

I'm still caught up in the feel of Sophie's warmth against me.

20 /
sophie

I STARE at myself in the mirror and think two things simultaneously.

The first is how much I absolutely love what Aimee has done to my hair.

The second is pure panic over what I'll tell my mother and how she'll react when I arrive home, driven by a boy she doesn't know, with pink hair.

It's not pink all over, just sections that peek out from underneath. But it's also very permanent.

Aimee sits in the chair beside me and twirls it to face me. We're in the salon she co-owns with another hairdresser. It's empty except for us, with all the other stylists finished for their Friday afternoon.

Aimee brought me here, sat me down and talked me through my colour choices, the picture I have saved on my phone open between us. Then she got to work, all the while chatting away, asking me about myself, telling me funny stories about Theo and Rhett. She talked about Asher, who's eight, and Ellie, who's thirteen, and sometimes she mentioned Dustin, mainly when she was telling me about some kind of trouble Rhett got himself into as a kid.

And now, a couple of hours later, I feel like there's a different person staring back at me from the mirror. As well as the colour, Aimee cut off several inches, so my hair now sits right above my shoulders, the ends choppy and blunt.

"I've texted Rhett. He's on his way with the kids," Aimee says, as casually as she has been this whole time about leaving her two kids in Rhett's care. She didn't think twice about trusting him with them, and it's settled the last of the nerves I had about trusting him myself.

"Thank you so much," I say, toying with the ends of my hair, the ones that are now candy-floss pink. "For doing this."

"You can stop thanking me, Sophie. It's no problem at all. I'd have done just about anything to get out of that arcade. It gives me such a headache."

I laugh, but it feels nervous.

There's no going back now.

I've committed to this hair colour; I've committed to the list.

The arcade felt like I was only testing the waters.

The hair colour feels like I've jumped in with both feet and now … now I want all the things on the list.

I mean, obviously I wanted them, or they wouldn't be on the list.

But now I want them with a burning desire.

I'm desperate to see who I am once I've ticked more things off.

Because although I'm anxious about how my new hair style is going to be received—by my mum, by Theo, by Rhett—I love it so much, and feel the most "me" I ever have.

The door bangs open and Asher bounds into the salon.

"Mum! Look what Rhett got me!" He shoves a giant stuffed monkey in Aimee's face.

I glance behind him, expecting Ellie and Rhett to be following Asher through the door. They're not, but then I catch a glimpse of them to the side of the building.

Rhett is hugging her, a hand smoothing across her hair. They pull apart and Rhett says something to her, bending down to look her in the eye as he does. She wipes at her face like she's wiping away tears, then nods and turns for the door.

I spin around, pretending I'm super interested in hearing Asher's recollection of everything he ate for dinner. I hear the sound of the door and smile at Rhett as he enters.

He stops. He stares.

I stand and face him, ready for him to laugh at me for wanting pink hair, to mock me for trying to be way cooler than I really am. Than I could ever be.

His eyes look a little red, his cheeks flushed, like his emotions are high. It makes sense after comforting his best friend's little sister, which I assume is what I just saw.

Rhett takes three steps towards me while I stand there and adjust my glasses, pushing them up my nose.

I want to say something clever and witty, but my voice won't work. His grey eyes are fixed on me and it all feels very intense. I want to run and hide.

"Your hair," he says eventually.

I reach up and grasp a handful of it, fiddling with the ends again. "Is it okay?" I whisper.

"Sweetheart." His voice goes soft as he reaches up and stills my hand, gently tugging it away from my hair. "Do *you* like it?"

I nod, unable to look away, unable to speak.

"That's what matters," he says. Then he grins at me, all his usual charm pouring back into his expression. "But for the record, I think it's awesome. I love it."

"Yeah?" I don't know why I'm still asking, but I am.

♥ 87

"Yes." He says it with such finality I know I won't be questioning it anymore. "I don't know what I was expecting, but it definitely wasn't this. It's so cool." He turns to Aimee. "Thank you so much."

Aimee shakes her head. "No, thank you for entertaining these two. I had the better part of this deal, for sure."

"Nah, these guys are all good," Rhett says, reaching out and wrapping an arm around Ellie, messing up her hair. She scowls and pulls away, but there's a tiny smile on her face. "Anytime, Aimee." They share a look and I get the feeling this whole evening has been more significant for Rhett and Dustin's family than I could possibly comprehend.

"Righto, you two," Aimee says to her kids. "Let's get you home. You, Rhett, don't be a stranger. I mean it."

"I promise," he says, the sincerity evident in his tone. "Come on, sweetheart," he says, turning back to me, "do you want more food before I take you home?"

"Yes, please," I say, grabbing my bag. "Thanks again, so much," I say to Aimee and she waves me off as we leave.

Right before the door clicks closed behind us I hear Asher's questioning voice. "I thought he said she wasn't his girlfriend?"

SOPHIE WON'T STOP FIDDLING with her hair and I can't decide if I love it or hate it.

Her nervous fiddling, not her hair. I love her hair.

It's shorter now, hanging above her shoulders, and there's little pink sections scattered throughout, which is kind of punk rock and also really sweet and adorable, so it's perfectly Sophie.

"Well, today hasn't exactly gone as I expected," I say as I pull into the carpark next to my favourite burger place.

"Sorry," Sophie says, leaning sideways in the passenger seat so she can face me. "I shouldn't have ditched you and left you with the kids."

"Oh, no, that's not what I meant," I say. "It was better than I expected. I am sorry I didn't get to hang out with you as much…" I trail off and the words linger in the space between us. My admission that I wanted to spend more time with her. But that shouldn't be unusual, or surprising. Of course I want to spend more time with her. We're friends. I'm helping her with her list. I clear my throat. "But it was really good to see Ellie and Asher again. It's been a while."

"Yeah?" She leaves the single word hanging, like it's an opening for me to talk more.

I nod. It's so easy to talk to Sophie like this, especially in the confines of the car, its doors and windows containing my secrets. The words spill out of me, words I've never said to anyone, words I never would say—except to Sophie. "I thought it was just Dusty, like, the reason I ever hung out with his family. I thought it was all about him. When he wasn't there anymore … I didn't feel like I fitted. But, I think, maybe I still do?"

It was so nice to see those kids again. I'd forgotten that it used to feel like they were my little siblings as well as Dusty's. I missed that feeling. I missed teasing Ellie and the way Asher always wanted to hang out with us, even when we really didn't want him to.

"Is Ellie okay?" Sophie's question pulls me back from my reminiscing. "I, uh, saw you outside the salon, right before you came in."

"Oh, yeah, she's okay. Like on the whole, she's okay. She pretty much didn't talk to me the whole time until we were right outside, by which point I'd obviously annoyed her enough for her to snap at me. She … she's pretty angry with me, for abandoning them." I hate the way my voice cracks as I say that. I hate even more that Ellie is right. I was so blinded by my own pain I forgot about theirs.

"You'll make it right, though?" Sophie's voice is so soft. There's no demand or accusation in it, just the subtle assurance that she believes I'll do the right thing.

"Yeah, I will."

We sit in the silence for several long minutes, looking at each other across the car. It's a terribly comfortable silence. I could bask in the warmth of it.

Her phone bleeps and it pulls her gaze away from me. I want

to reach out and lift her chin, bringing her focus back to me, never leaving this moment.

She sighs as she reads the message, then taps out a reply.

"Do you need to get home?" I ask. My voice is rough, like I've forgotten how to use it.

She shakes her head. "Nah, not yet. But I shouldn't be out too much later."

"All right. Food time," I say, and push open the car door. The cool evening air sneaks in and dispels the last of the soft, cosy moment we shared a minute ago.

We order food and perch on a couple of tall stools to wait. Sophie fiddles with her hair some more while I play with a salt packet.

"I have a couple of ideas for other things to tick off," I say, watching her trail her fingers through the pink sections of hair. "But I'll have to figure some stuff out first."

"You don't have to," she says abruptly. "We don't have to do this."

"What do you mean?"

"The list. You don't have to help me. It's really stupid."

I blink at her. Once, twice, three times, before my brain catches up. "You want to give up?"

"No," she says and shrugs. "It's … it's really dumb. I should be able to do these things without asking for your help. There's nothing on there I can't do … but I'm too scared. It's pathetic and I shouldn't have pulled you into it. We can forget about it."

"Um, no. I'm fully invested in this list now. I have plans. You aren't ruining my plans."

She laughs, and I feel so gratified. I didn't know how good it would make me feel to make her laugh, especially when she's clearly in the process of getting down on herself about who she is.

"Sorry, didn't realise this was all about you." Her eyes sparkle with amusement.

"Obviously it is," I say. "Rude of you to assume it's not. Isn't everything about me?"

"This is very, very true." She's laughing—with me, at me, I don't care which. Her hands have dropped from her hair and haven't returned, like she's forgotten to be nervous about it.

"Are you worried how your mum will react to your hair?" Oh, my stupid big mouth. Way to ruin everything.

Sophie sighs, props her elbow on the table and rests her head on her hand. "Yeah, a little bit. But it's too late now."

"A little." I hold up my thumb and finger a hair's breadth apart. "Tell her the colour's temporary. Then by the time she realises it's not she'll have realised how awesome it is and won't care anymore."

"Yeah, except then she'll know I lied to her and she'll be mad about that. I dunno, guess I just have to deal with it. I have to tell Theo too, without, like, giving away the whole list thing."

Ah, I hadn't thought of Theo yet. And no doubt Aimee will mention something to them at some point. I wonder if I should text her and ask her to not say anything.

"All right, well obviously we need a cover story that doesn't involve lying," I say, taking a moment to think it over. "The truth is actually fairly reasonable, if you don't mention the list. Tell Theo I dragged you to the arcade because I had a craving for their loaded fries, which I did. Then you can tell them we saw Aimee and the kids and that you mentioned dyeing your hair and Aimee offered. Which is pretty much exactly what happened."

Sophie studies me for a long moment. "I suppose you're right."

"I usually am, sweetheart."

MY MUM IS SITTING at the kitchen table drawing when Rhett drops me home.

He's promised to text me as soon as he has firm plans in place for ticking off the next item on my list. Despite my protests, he's still fully committed to checking off as many items as possible. I think he's more invested in it than I am.

I close the front door behind me and take a moment to lean against it. I need just a little more time wrapped up in the cosy bubble of feelings from tonight. Despite all that happened, from the arcade to my makeover, my mind keeps lingering on the moment Rhett saw my hair, his warm fingers lingering against my skin as he asked if I liked it, then told me he loved it, even though his opinion doesn't matter.

Mum glances up from the picture she's working on when I enter the kitchen. I'm so busy thinking about Rhett's grin and the way he calls me sweetheart—which is infuriating and at the same time makes my stomach do little flips—I almost forget to be nervous about her reaction to my hair. Almost.

I slide into a seat at the table and pick up a finished picture, hoping if I act like everything is totally normal she won't lose her mind. I study the coloured pencil drawing of a bouquet of flowers, and like all of my mum's drawings, it's gorgeous.

"Oh, I love this one," I say.

She's staring at me. "Your hair," she says eventually, and her voice is rough, like she's had trouble speaking.

I think back to the moment Rhett saw it, the way he said it only mattered that I loved it. I try to remember the feeling I had in that moment, when I felt the most like myself I ever had. "Um, yeah. A friend did it." At Mum's stricken look, I continue. "She's a hairdresser. Like has a salon and everything. It wasn't Theo doing it in the bathroom."

Mum's expression softens slightly, but not by much.

"What are you going to do about school?"

"Nothing. Hair colour isn't stipulated in the dress code. They can't do anything about it. We checked before we did it." Plenty of other kids at school have coloured hair, but Aimee still made me check the actual policy.

Mum picks up a pink pencil, puts it down again then selects a yellow one. It's like she's making a point of not looking at me.

"I really like it," I say, my voice wavering far more than I'd like. "I'm sorry if it doesn't meet your approval. I'm going to bed," I add before she has time to respond. "Good night."

I scoop my school bag off the floor and head for my room.

That went better than I expected. At least she didn't yell, or give me that really disappointed look she's so good at. She didn't tell me I have to change it back, ground me or confiscate my phone—not that she's ever really been that kind of parent.

I suppose she could still come up with some kind of repercussion and dish it out tomorrow, once she's had time to process.

I get ready for bed, scrubbing the make-up off my face, brushing my teeth and pulling on my comfiest pyjamas, then flop onto my bed.

I grab my phone and send Theo a text.

SOPHIE:

Theo, I did a thing.

Their response comes so fast it's like they've been waiting all night for my message.

THEO:

You kissed Rhett didn't you?

I almost drop my phone on my face.

SOPHIE:

WHAT? NO!

Theo sends me back a crying face emoji. Is that what they thought today was? A date?

My stomach drops even though I'm lying down. I didn't know that was a thing that could happen.

Was it a date? And I was the only one who didn't know?

SOPHIE:

Why are you crying?

THEO:

Because either you're lying to me, did kiss him and won't tell me about it. Or you didn't kiss him, in which case I'm sad for you.

Because you totally should have.

SOPHIE:

It's not like that Theo.

My phone rings, Theo's face appearing on the screen with the incoming call. I don't want to answer it, but considering Theo knows I'm right here with my phone in hand I can't really ignore the call.

"Hi, Theo," I say. At least it's only a voice call and not a video one showing off my hair in all its glory.

"I don't know where to start with you," they say. "With the alleged not kissing Rhett or the thing you were going to tell me about."

"Since there's nothing to talk about to do with Rhett, I'd suggest the thing I messaged to actually tell you about."

"Okay, I'm gonna let the Rhett thing slide for now. What's the thing you did?"

I exhale and relax into my pillows. I'm not sure I've got a permanent reprieve from Theo's enthusiasm for something happening between me and Rhett, but I'll take whatever I can get for now. I still need time to unpack all the feelings I have about Rhett Carmichael.

"Hang on one sec," I tell Theo, then tap into my camera roll and send a photo to them through messages. "I've sent you a pic."

A moment later I hear Theo's message sound chirp. There's dead silence for another moment.

"Oh. My. God." Theo says. "This is amazing. Do you love it?"

I laugh. "Yeah, yeah I do."

"Why didn't you tell me?" A few beats of silence. "Soph, is there something going on between us that I haven't noticed? Is everything okay?"

"Everything is fine, Theo. I promise."

"It's only that, well … I could have got someone to do this for you. My aunt, she's got a salon. I could have come with you and like, cheered you on when you tried to freak out about it … and you went with Rhett Carmichael, of all people."

"It's kind of a weird story. And it wasn't a planned thing," I say. "And as it turns out, it was your aunt who did it."

"Wait. What? How?"

I take a deep breath and launch into the story, leaving out any references to my stupid, dorky list, but telling them about seeing Aimee, Ellie and Asher at the arcade and how Rhett babysat the kids while Aimee did my hair.

"And you didn't kiss him after all that?"

"Theo! No! There was no kissing."

"But guys don't go round babysitting kids so a platonic friend can get a deal on hair colour."

"Apparently Rhett does. And they weren't any random kids. I think he wanted to hang out with them. I think he probably needed to."

Theo goes quiet for a few breaths. "You know what, I think you're right about that."

"MORNING," I say as Grandad shuffles into the kitchen. "Want coffee?"

Grandad eyes me suspiciously. I can't really blame him. I'm up first this morning, on a Saturday when I don't have to be. Not only am I awake, but I'm in a good mood. I smile at him and I swear he flinches.

"Please," he says.

We sit at the table across from each other like usual, drinking our coffee, him with a bowl of boring bran cereal and me with peanut butter on toast and thinking about my plans to achieve the next item on Sophie's list.

"What's up with you?"

"Hmm? What do you mean?" I ask, my planning interrupted.

"You're in a good mood. You're humming. It's not even 7 am on a Saturday. You feeling okay?" Grandad's voice is gruff, but he's joking.

"Haha," I say. "I am a fully functioning human, you know."

"Good to know," he says. "What'd you do last night?"

I try really hard not to be immediately defensive. I don't think he's being confrontational.

"I hung out with Sophie for a little while and then with Ellie and Asher at the arcade."

"Ellie and Asher?" Recognition flicks across his face but it's obvious he can't place the names.

"Yeah, they're, um, Dusty's little brother and sister."

He's quiet for a moment. The only sounds are the clink of his spoon against his bowl and the crunching of my chewing, which suddenly seems way too loud for this moment.

"I was going to go do the lawns at home this morning," I say after I swallow. "Is that okay?"

"Yeah, Rhett, that's okay."

For the first time since I got stuck here, I don't feel like I'm on the edge of a cliff where one wrong move will send me plummeting. This conversation, as stilted as it is, is actually … nice?

"I can do yours afterwards if you like."

"Well, that's better than okay. I'd really appreciate it."

"All right then. Can you let me know when Grandma is going to the book fair? I'll try and be done by then so I can go with her."

He nods as I push back from the table and take my plate to the dishwasher. This is the longest conversation we've had since I moved in and he goaded me the first night, and the first time I don't feel angry and resentful in his presence. It makes a nice change, but I wonder how long it'll last.

I PUSH the lawn mower back and forth for hours, leaving me a sweaty mess and my arms feeling like jelly from the constant vibrations of the mower, but the lawns at home and at my grandparents' are done.

Grandma went in for an early stint at the book fair, so I missed her, but I've offered to pick her up. After I shower I climb back in my car and head for the warehouse.

I walk in the door and my gaze is drawn straight to one person.

Sophie.

As usual she's surrounded by stacks of books, chatting to Tonya as she sorts, the sunlight glinting off her hair.

She glances up and grins as she catches sight of me. I smile and wave.

Tonya gives me a look as I approach, but I don't know how to decipher it. Before I have a chance to ask she says hello, then excuses herself to go and help someone else.

"Hey," Sophie says, looking up at me with those big brown eyes.

"Hey," I say and fall into a seat beside her. "How did it go with your mum?"

She shrugs, and her smiley disposition dips a little. "It was fine. Theo likes it, though."

"I'm not surprised. Theo has good taste."

"You think so?" She looks at me as though she can't tell if I'm joking or not.

"Of course. They're friends with you." I reach out and tug at a lock of pink hair. She laughs and blushes, half-heartedly pushing my hand away.

I've spent pretty much the entirety of the past twenty-four hours thinking about this girl, replaying all our interactions in my head. I don't think she's ever looked as pretty as she does in this moment, spring sunshine highlighting pink hair and rosy heat on her cheeks. She's wearing that fuzzy pink cardigan again, the one from the first day I met her, and the whole look is so adorable I want to switch my playful touch into something else entirely.

I clear my throat and push that thought away.

"Do you have plans this afternoon?"

She shakes her head and gestures at the piles of books around her. "Only more of this and some avoiding of my mother."

"Oof, was it that bad?"

"It wasn't bad … but it wasn't great, either. It was fine. But I don't want to keep reminding her of it. Besides, if I don't see her she can't dole out some kind of punishment."

"That's going to be pretty hard unless you avoid her for a really long time."

She laughs again. "Yeah, but after a little while she'll get used to it. It won't be a big deal anymore. Anyway, why do you ask?"

Ask? Oh, about her plans.

"I've got some more things to tick off your list. And the ideal window is in about two hours."

She slides another three books onto a pile. She hasn't stopped sorting the entire time we've been talking, while all I can do is sit here and stare at her.

"If you're up for it," I say, trying to tease her into saying yes. I don't know where the thought comes from, but I realise I'll be really disappointed if she says no, especially after saying she didn't have specific plans.

"I told you, we don't have to do the list anymore," she says, her voice soft. She won't meet my eyes.

"Sweetheart, I told you, I'm committed now. Come on, you want to do these things, yeah?" I use a single finger to reach out and tip her chin up so she can't avoid eye contact.

"Yeah," she murmurs, and the enormous warehouse full of books and people disappears. In this moment, it's only me and Sophie and the single point of contact where my fingertip touches her chin.

"Then we'll do what we can, okay? It'll be fun. I promise." The words cause something to unsettle in my gut, but I ignore the feeling and the memory they conjure. "Are you with me?"

She holds my gaze for the longest moment, eyes serious on mine, and I'm about to admit defeat, to drop my hand and turn away, when she finally speaks.

"Yeah," she says, a smile touching her lips. "I'm in."

I breathe a huge, joyful sigh of relief and force myself to lower my hand, breaking contact with her face, even though it's the very last thing I want to do.

24 /
sophie

RHETT SITS with me and sorts books.

He's easily distracted though, and repeatedly interrupts my sorting to ask me if I've read a particular book and if I thought it was any good.

He holds up a near-perfect-condition paperback of one of my favourite romance books ever. "Well, this looks cheesy," he says, and I feel my face flush.

"Nope," I say, grabbing the book from him and sliding it onto a pile. I'm tempted to claim it for myself, but I do already have a copy at home. "No more judging books. Just sort."

"Ooh," he sing-songs. "Did I hit a nerve? Are you a … what do they call it? A romance girlie?"

"To be honest, I thought that was fairly obvious, and I'm concerned about your perceptions of the world if you haven't noticed that by now."

"Concerned about me, huh?"

He's incorrigible. I roll my eyes. "Just a tiny bit. Now, work." I tap the pile of books in front of him.

WHEN WE'RE DONE with sorting—well, I'm beginning to wonder if we'll ever actually be done, but we're done for now—we drop Rhett's grandma off at home.

"I should be home by dinner," he tells her. "But I'll let you know if Sophie keeps me out later."

"Don't you go falling for his nonsense," she says to me.

I shake my head. "Never."

But I'm pretty sure it's a lie. I'm pretty sure I've already fallen for his nonsense.

I didn't matter how hard I concentrated on the stacks of books I was sorting, my mind kept lingering on that moment when he'd tilted my chin up and made me meet his eyes.

My mind was particularly fond of the moment right before he broke contact, when for one hopeful second I thought maybe he wasn't going to pull away.

Rhett seems completely oblivious to my thought spiral, which I guess is a good thing, because I'm not sure I want him to know these thoughts.

Or the other thoughts I have about him. Like how his eyes look like a stormy day at the beach—one I'd love to be swept up in, or how I'd really like to touch his hair, or maybe more importantly, how desperate I am for him to touch me. To take his casual, platonic affection and turn it into something else.

Instead of him ruffling my hair, I want him to thread his fingers through it.

Rather than lifting my chin, I want his fingertip to trace my face and his palm to cup my cheek.

The casual throwing of his arm around my shoulders can turn into him sliding a hand around my waist and pulling me close.

I like romance books because fiction is often so much better than the reality. But with Rhett, I think I'd like the reality.

It all feels like some wild pipe dream that's so far removed from my actual life, though.

That Rhett Carmichael would be into the boring, shy girl who sorts books for fun.

But Theo ... Theo doesn't seem to think it's unlikely. Theo seems to think it's a sure thing.

The trouble with being the boring, shy girl is that I don't have experience with this kind of thing. I don't know how to find out what Rhett's feeling—not without throwing myself out there and baring my soul.

People are too hard. That's why I stick with books.

And Theo, because they didn't really give me a choice about being friends. Not that I'd ever regret them forcing their love on me.

Rhett drives a few blocks. We don't talk, which is probably good because my thoughts are too busy running wild.

It's not a long drive, then Rhett parks on a street I've never been down. The house he's stopped outside looks pretty much like every other one on the street: suburban homes with tidy front lawns and tall timber fences dividing the sections.

"Come on," he says, climbing out of the car and gesturing for me to follow him.

I do, but my steps slow when he bypasses the front door to the house. He skirts around the edge of the garage, glancing back over his shoulder at me, then at the street. There are no cars in the driveway, and I stumble as realisation hits me.

Rhett's arm shoots out and catches me before I fall flat on my face.

"Rhett," I hiss. "What are you doing? Are we supposed to be here?"

He grins down at me and slides his hand down my arm, lacing his fingers with mine and tugging me forward.

Now I'm really freaking out because A. I'm pretty sure we're breaking into this property, which I really don't want to do, and B. Rhett is holding my hand, and that feeling might make me follow him anywhere.

"Come on," he says, reaching a gate that screens off the backyard. Another quick glance around and he reaches through to lift the latch and push it open. He pulls me through the gap and pushes the gate closed, leaning back against it.

"Rhett, are we supposed to be here?"

"Supposed to be? Yes …"

"Are we allowed to be here?"

I receive a grin in response.

He's still holding my hand, and instead of replying he lifts his arm, spinning me so my back is against his front, his arm wrapping across my stomach, still holding my hand even though the manoeuvre gave him every opportunity to let go when our grip slipped. I suck in a breath and try not to pass out from the dizzying effect of his touch on me.

"Two things on your list," he whispers into my ear. "What are they?"

I can't think. Not with me wrapped up in him like this, his voice low in my ear.

I force myself to focus, to take in the back yard in front of me. Stunning gardens fringe the edges, a patio barbecue area and a huge in-ground swimming pool.

"Umm …" Words have abandoned me. Rhett's body is so warm.

He chuckles. "Think about it," he says.

"Umm … swimming?" I ask and feel the movement of his head as he nods.

"And? Why are you so freaked out right now?"

I'm pretty sure he's not referring to my freaking out that his hand on my belly, his mouth beside my ear, and how close he's holding me right now.

"Breaking ... breaking the rules?"

"Got it," he says, and I can imagine the look on his face; that self-assured cocky grin and wicked glint in his eye. "Shall we?"

"Shall we what?"

"Swim, sweetheart."

He releases me, and by the time I've recovered enough to turn to face him, he's already shucking his jacket. He reaches for his t-shirt and pulls it over his head.

"Come on," he says. "You wanted it to be spontaneous."

I gulp.

You have got to be freaking kidding me.

25 /
rhett

SOPHIE STANDS a metre away from me, gaping.

I want to close the space between us and have her in my arms again.

Instead, I drop my t-shirt onto a patio chair along with my jacket and raise a challenging eyebrow at her. "You gonna bail on me, sweetheart?"

She opens and closes her mouth like a goldfish, and I grin down at her.

"You didn't think this through at all, huh?" she asks, voice so thick and raspy I almost can't make out the words.

"Sure I did. You wanted spontaneous, though. Now come on." I flick the button on my jeans and slip them off, then take a running jump for the pool.

Sophie's face is already flaming; she might combust if I spend too long standing around in underwear.

The water rushes around my head as I fully submerge and when I surface, flicking the water out of my hair and eyes, Sophie hasn't moved, except to turn to face the pool.

"It's heated, if that's what's holding you up," I say. It's still too early in the year for appropriate swimming weather, but this pool is good any time of the year. Despite what Sophie says, I did think this through.

"What am I supposed to wear?" She mumbles the words, so I can barely hear her over the water lapping the edge of the pool.

"Whatever you want," I say. "The point is not to think too much about it."

She hesitates, then shrugs off her cardigan and drops it onto the pile of my clothes. Her t-shirt follows, and she's standing in front of me in jeans and a tank top. She kicks off her shoes.

That's as far as she gets before freezing. After a long moment of her looking anywhere but at me, our eyes meet and lock.

She looks desperate and terrified.

"Sophie," I say, and her eyes close slowly. "Sweetheart, you don't have to do anything you don't want to. It's your choice."

I turn away to give her a moment, swimming a few strokes from the edge of the pool before diving under. I used to be able to hold my breath for a really long time. It's been a while since I tried, but now seems as good a time as any to test my abilities.

I've counted to forty-two when the water explodes around me. I startle and shoot to the surface, gasping as my head breaks through.

A bedraggled Sophie is treading water beside me. Her hair is plastered to her head and she's spluttering like she's cold. Under the surface I can make out a lot of exposed skin and a bright purple strap crosses each shoulder.

Okay. She's right. I did not think this through.

Not before I brought her here, not while I was taking off my own clothes, not even while she was hesitating over taking off her own.

And now I'm swimming with Sophie, who's also only wearing underwear.

"You made it," I say, my voice thick and hoarse.

She smiles at me. It's shy and hesitant, like when she showed me her hair last night. I can't believe that was only last night.

And here she is again, clearly excited but too scared to show it.

"You know I wouldn't have thought any less of you if you hadn't done this, right?" I say.

"Yeah, right," Sophie says with an eye roll. "You would have mocked me relentlessly."

"Oh, absolutely. But it doesn't mean I would think less of who you are. Sticking to your boundaries is totally badass, sweetheart."

She stands neck deep in the water, clearly having an internal battle with herself over something, but she got in the pool, so now I need to make her spontaneous swim something worth remembering.

I splash some water in her direction, hoping to break through her tension. She recoils then faces me again, a wicked grin on her face. That's more like it.

She points a finger at me. "Don't start."

"I already did." I splash her again and she yelps, then retaliates. We chase each other around the pool until I hold up both hands in surrender. Sophie leans against the side of the pool, her breath coming in gasps.

"I can't believe we broke in and used this random person's pool," she says, a troubled expression creeping into her eyes.

I heave myself out of the water and head for the house, searching through the garden beside the back door.

"I kind of maybe exaggerated that part of it," I say as I slip the key I've found into the lock.

I glance back at her. She's gaping at me again, and I don't know if it's indignation about my sort-of lie or because I'm standing here soaking wet in my underwear. I'm not sure which would be better, to be honest.

Right inside the door there's a cupboard, and I open it and grab two towels. I wrap myself in one then head back to the edge of the pool where Sophie is waiting. I drop a towel beside her then return to lock the door and hide the key, giving her a moment to get out of the pool and wrap herself in the towel.

Before I get a chance to lock the door, someone appears from the other side of the room. She waves and I pull the door open again.

"I'll be right back," I say over my shoulder to Sophie, who's looking startled and like she's about to be in huge amounts of trouble. "It's all good, sweetheart," I say, then step inside to say hello to Aimee.

"Glad you could make it," she says with a smile.

"Thanks for letting us use the pool."

"Rhett, honey, you can use it anytime. You don't need to ask. Whenever you want, and you can come by anytime too."

"Thanks, Aimee."

"Now, you'd both better go put something warm on before you freeze to death. I'm not being held responsible for that."

I laugh and rub at my arms that are prickled with goose-bumps. I thank her again and head back outside. She locks the door and waves at Sophie, who gives a timid wave back.

"This is Aimee's place?" she asks.

"Ah, yeah. Technically there were no rules broken … but in my defence—" The rest of the words I was planning to say evaporate straight out of my head. They're simply vaporised.

Sophie is wearing my jacket. She's wrapped the towel around her body and slipped my jacket over the top.

But it's not actually my jacket. It's Dusty's. I inherited it from him.

Three steps are all it takes for me to be standing right in front of her. I don't know what I'm doing, but I take both sides of the jacket hem in my hands and hold her there.

Her breath comes in short gasps, the way it did earlier when I held her close to me, her back to my front. Her brown eyes gaze up from behind her glasses, which I'd missed while we were swimming.

I tug at the jacket, pulling her hips closer to mine.

"Look at you," I whisper. "You're going to kill me, sweetheart."

Then I force myself to let her go.

26 /
sophie

RHETT STEPS away from me and starts flinging his clothes on so fast I stand there blinking for several minutes, or years, maybe, before my brain catches up.

He didn't kiss me.

I was sure he was going to.

That was after the moment I thought he was going to be mad because I'd borrowed his jacket. When he first saw me I wasn't sure how he was going to react. A collection of emotions played across his face before settling into this super-intense look in his eyes.

He grabbed the jacket and pulled me to him, close enough that the fronts of our thighs were touching and I thought it was happening.

The first kiss.

My first kiss.

But apparently not, because now he's dressed and watching me, waiting for me.

I begin to slide the jacket off my shoulders, but he shakes his head. "It's okay. Keep it for now. Don't get cold. Bring the towel, too. I'll bring it back another time." He gestures to the gate. "Come on, I'd better get you home."

He's so detached, like this whole afternoon didn't happen— the hand holding, wrapping his arm around my waist and holding me against him, chasing each other around the pool. Every moment our bodies collided underwater and I realised how much skin I had exposed, but that I never felt nervous or shy or awkward. Then the whole thing with the jacket and him whispering in a hoarse voice that I was going to kill him.

It's like all those tiny moments have been erased.

Rhett is distant, acting like he can't wait to get out of here and far away from me. I'm feeling far more awkward in this moment than when I was in the pool with him in my bright purple bra.

I grab my pile of clothes, hugging them to my body, unsure if I feel numb from the cold air or Rhett's cold shoulder. I shove my feet into my shoes and hurry out the gate he's holding open for me.

We walk back to the car in silence and climb inside. Rhett blasts the heater. He drives me back to my car, the air in his warm and toasty in one way and the opposite in another.

Everyone is gone from the warehouse and my car is sitting alone on the side of the street.

I go to remove the jacket again, but Rhett stops me, placing a hand on my arm.

"I'll grab it off you next time I see you."

"You sure?" I'm relieved. I don't want to part with it yet. I shouldn't have any kind of attachment to it, but I want to sit for a little bit longer, wrapped in his clothes.

Rhett nods. The look on his face tugs at my heart. He looks like he wants to tell me something painful, but he can't find the words. I twist my arm so his hand that's resting on my sleeve falls into my palm. I squeeze softly.

"Thank you, Rhett," I say softly. "That was fun."

He opens his mouth to say something, but doesn't. He nods instead.

"I'll see you Monday," I say, since apparently I'm the only one having this conversation. I try not to be angry about it.

He nods again and I climb out of the car, heading for my own.

As I drive away, Rhett stays parked on the side of the road.

I want to go back. I want to shake the thoughts in his head loose, have him tell me what's going on and why he suddenly pulled away and closed off.

Instead, I head straight for Theo's house.

I park in the driveway and Theo appears on the path leading to the backyard.

"Hey," they say, clearly surprised by my unannounced visit. I usually text before showing up.

I close my car door and Theo gives me an up-and-down look, taking in my bedraggled hair, my smudged mascara and the jacket and towel I'm still wearing.

"Oh … Come on, help me pull weeds."

"I—What? Did you say pull weeds?"

Theo nods and gestures for me to follow. In the backyard it looks like a garden massacre is going down. Weeds and plant offcuts are dumped in haphazard piles and a selection of gardening tools are scattered across the lawn. It's obvious where Theo has got up to with the weeding, the garden going from tidy to wildly overgrown in one exact spot.

Theo tosses me a pair of gardening gloves then immediately starts ripping things out of the garden. I kneel next to them in my towel and oversized denim jacket, but don't start murdering plants.

"What happened?" Theo asks, grunting as they fight with a particularly stubborn plant.

I let out a long breath. "I really like him," I whisper, as if this is some secret Theo doesn't already know. I haven't said it in as many words, but Theo knows. Theo always knows these things.

They give up on the weeds and sit cross-legged, facing me, waiting for me. I guess the only response they could give to that statement is, "Yeah, I know."

"He ... he doesn't feel the same way."

At that, Theo raises both eyebrows and leans back on their hands. "Evidence, please."

"We hung out after book sorting. He took me to your aunt's place. We went swimming."

Theo rolls their eyes. "That part's pretty obvious, Soph."

I manage to crack a smile.

"Wait," they say. "What did you swim in? Do you carry emergency swimwear in your car?"

I roll my eyes and the tiniest laugh escapes. "No, Theo, I do not carry emergency swimwear. I—uh, didn't swim in very much."

"Sophie!" I feel like I need to rub my ears after the volume and pitch of Theo's yelp. "Did you go skinny dipping in my aunt's pool in the middle of the day?"

My face flames. I bet it's bright red at this point. "No. Not exactly. What even is the definition of skinny dipping? Is it totally naked? Which didn't happen. Anyway, that's not the point."

"No, it's really not, but I think total nudity is the requirement for skinny dipping. But I digress. Continue."

"We had a moment ... I guess. I thought that maybe something was going to happen." I fiddle with the worn cuff of the jacket. "But then he pulled away and virtually didn't talk to me again. So ..." I let out another heavy breath. "Turns out he doesn't like me." I give a hopeless little shrug and will the tears filling my eyes not to fall. It feels extremely dumb to cry over a boy I barely know.

Theo makes a thinking noise. "I don't think that means he doesn't like you. I think it means he's a bit of a messed-up guy who saw the girl he really does like wearing that jacket, and it probably fritzed his brain a bit."

"What do you mean?"

"That jacket, Soph. Seeing you wearing it might have … I dunno." They shrug. "Maybe triggered something for him."

"Why?" My voice is a whisper. I knew something happened in the moment he saw me in it, but with what happened directly afterwards, it was easy to forget.

"Soph, it was Dusty's."

BEFORE SOPHIE'S car even turns the corner at the end of the street, I'm banging my fist against my steering wheel.

I shout and curse at myself and when my hand begins to ache, I rest my forehead against the battered wheel.

I've completely messed everything up.

Again.

I start the car. I should go home, back to my grandparents'. I should, but I don't. Instead, I find myself heading for the lookout.

It's a sunny Saturday afternoon so it's busy, but there's one free parking spot right down the end. I slip into the shade of the tree that hides the trail to Dusty's spot, and a few moments later the sea breeze is hitting my face.

I take my first deep breath since I saw Sophie in that jacket.

I don't know if Sophie is mad at me, or something else. I don't *think* she's mad, but I got so locked up in my own head that I probably wouldn't have noticed even if she started throwing things at me. She's not that type of person, so maybe I totally overlooked her rage.

I think she's more likely confused and maybe a little hurt. Okay, a lot hurt.

It's pretty obvious, even to me, that we had a moment. It's not the first moment we've had like that, either. We've had so many perfect little moments, all leading up to that one.

The one where I should have pulled her even closer and kissed her.

I lean my shoulder against a rock as I sit on the edge of the cliff. It's not much of a cliff and if I were to fall it'd hurt, but I probably wouldn't be too broken. It's only a few metres down to a paddock. Sure, there're a few rocks down there at the bottom of the cliff, but it's not like a sheer drop to the ocean or anything.

I close my eyes, smell the ocean and think about what kissing Sophie would be like. I let myself sink into those thoughts, those feelings, for a few minutes, imagining the sensation of her lips against mine, her fingers in my hair.

Then I snap myself out of it.

I pulled away from her for a reason, and it wasn't because I didn't think she wanted me there. That's the worst part of all this. I've hurt her as well.

But for her own good.

Her list was pretty specific about how she wanted her first kiss to go. *A first kiss under the stars.* I didn't want to take that moment from her. She didn't ask for it to be the middle of the afternoon while my dead best friend's mum watched us from the window and she shivered from the cold because I'd made her go swimming way too early in the year.

There was that, but there was also all the things Renee said last year when she dumped me. I don't usually put much stock in my ex-girlfriend's opinion of me. Well, at least I thought I didn't.

But in that moment with Sophie, when I remembered the item written on her list surrounded by tiny hand-drawn stars, I knew that if I did what I really wanted to do, I'd be everything Renee had accused me of.

Self-involved.

Selfish.

Completely oblivious to anyone but myself.

The worst thing is that she was right. About all of it.

Of course, I didn't see it at the time. My best friend was dead. I was supposed to be upset. Renee was totally wrong about me being so self-involved I couldn't see that other people were hurting, that I was hurting other people.

It took a literal fire for me to wake up.

Even then I was still resentful. Resentful that I had to live a life without Dusty in it. Resentful that Renee ended our relationship.

And sure, the fire made me realise that I needed to sort myself out, but when I finally looked up and realised there was no one I could turn to anymore, that I was alone, the resentment didn't fully go away.

Especially after my parents revoked their trust in letting me stay at home while they went on their trip.

But it worked out for the best. I have to admit that.

Because staying with my grandparents isn't so bad, even if Grandad is a stereotypical grumpy old man.

If I hadn't been staying with them and been forced into book-sorting labour, I'd never have spent more than a couple of minutes with Sophie.

A couple of minutes during which I'd been my usual snarky self. I cringe at the memory. Definitely not my finest moment.

But somehow, in the short time I've known her, I've lost that bitter edge of resentment I was holding on to.

And in that time I've been an even bigger jerk than that first time we met in the library, and she's still forgiven me.

It feels like I'm at another crossroads, right here in this moment. I can do the easy thing and let whatever we have slip away, let Sophie move on with her life and maybe one day look back on this little blip of friendship with fondness.

The edge of the sun dips behind the trees behind me and I'm plunged into shadow, and I realise that ghosting Sophie isn't actually the easy route.

Staying away from her isn't easy. Only being able to watch from afar as she laughs with Theo during lunchtime, or even more endearingly, watching her reading while Theo sits right next to her and listens to music, the pair not speaking at all. That's not easy either.

Letting her finish her list without me. Definitely not easy.

I'm going to have to stop being all those things Renee called me. I'm going to have to fight the urge to fall back into all that.

It's also not easy. It's going to be hard and I'm probably going to screw it up.

But I'm going to try to make things right.

It won't be easy but it's what Sophie deserves.

28 /
sophie

MONDAY MORNING and I'm back in my happy place.

The library has that perfect, peaceful quiet to it, while everywhere outside students are catching up after the weekend, loudly reliving whatever it is they got up to.

I'm appreciating the solitude and the relaxing rhythm of shelving books.

Unfortunately all this peace and quiet is giving me a lot of time to think about Rhett and what Theo said about him over the weekend. Even after the disastrous end to Saturday's swim, Theo hasn't given up on the potential of a romantic future between me and Rhett. I'm sceptical, but the ball's in his court at this point.

Theo's revelation about the origins of the jacket makes a lot of sense, so maybe that moment by the pool was simply Rhett's emotional reaction to seeing me wearing it.

I surprised him. He was overwhelmed. Then realised what was happening and ended it before we could do anything that was impossible to reverse.

I'm disappointed and maybe feel a touch burned that he didn't want to kiss me, but I get it. I just really hope our fledgeling friendship can survive yet another hurdle.

I slide more books onto the shelf, then hear the front door of the library open. I peer around the end of a stack as Rhett walks into the room, looking towards the checkout counter then around the library when he sees the desk vacant.

He has a book in his hand. Maybe he's come to return it.

I hesitate, wondering if I should go over and take the book from him. I wonder if I should pull the next book in the series from under the desk where I stashed it this morning when I scanned it back into the system, and offer to check it out for him.

"Hey," he says as his eyes land on me. I guess any decision I had to make is now redundant. He waves the book. "I, uh, came to get the next one."

"You're finished already?" I ask, even though it's a stupid question, because obviously he has if he wants the next one.

"Yeah," he says. "Didn't have much on yesterday." He might be blushing. It's kind of cute.

I really wish I didn't think that. I wish I didn't look at him and have my heart do big, swooping somersaults in my chest. I wish I could look at him the way I did a week ago, when we were barely friends, before the list and the hair and the swimming.

"The next one came back this morning," I say, wheeling my book shelving cart over to the desk and pulling the battered paperback out from its hiding spot. "I put it aside for you."

He blinks for a few moments, as though he's surprised by my gesture. "Thanks," he says.

"I have the jacket and the towel in my car, too. I didn't want to carry them around all day, so if you meet me after school?"

"Yeah, yeah, of course." He still looks like he's surprised by my behaviour. I'm not sure how he was expecting me to act. Was I supposed to be yelling? Crying? Totally ignoring him?

Maybe the last one, because it kind of felt like that on Saturday when he dropped me off.

But I don't want that. I don't want bad feelings to linger. I want to dissolve the awkwardness and get on with being friends.

If he wanted something more I wouldn't say no ... but if friendship is all that's on the table, then I want it.

"About ..." Rhett trails off almost immediately, then takes a deep breath and pushes through. "About Saturday, I wanted to apologise. I'm sorry for how I acted. You deserve better than that. I ... have some things going on in my head. But I truly am sorry."

"Rhett," I say, after his voice trails off for a second time, but this time instead of trying again he looks at me with such sincere apology and pleading in his eyes I know he's done talking.

Something flickered in his face when I said his name, and I wonder if I've ever said it to his face before. I kind of like the way it feels on my tongue, I like the way it caused his features to jolt in the tiniest way.

"It's okay." I step closer to him. He's placed his book on the counter. When I place mine beside it, I try very hard not to notice how close our hands are to touching. "I know you've got stuff going on. It's okay."

Relief floods him. He exhales and his shoulders drop. I hadn't realised how tense he was until it falls away. "Thank you. I'm so relieved to hear that."

"Of course. What did you think I was going to say? We're friends, aren't we?"

I don't know why I say those words. I don't know why I'm pretty much asking him point-blank to lock me into his friend zone.

"I really hope so," he says, his voice soft. "The things going on in my head ... I'd really like to tell you, but they're the kinds of things I'd only ever tell a friend."

My breath catches and my heart leaps into my throat on its next somersault. He wants to tell me these things? That's far more than I was anticipating. I smile up at him, his grey eyes light today, like polished silver.

"I'd really like that," I say. "But only if you want to tell me. You don't have to, even if we are friends."

"Yeah, I know. But I figured since I know all your secrets, we should be on even footing." He grins down at me, the gentle, slightly hesitant smile from a second ago morphing back into his usual carefree one. "Don't ya think so, sweetheart?"

I roll my eyes and punch him in the arm.

"Ow," he says with a laugh, rubbing at the spot.

"Oh, hardly." I punch him again. I'm pretty sure it's hurting me more than it's hurting him.

"Watch it, sweetheart," he says, then grabs my wrists and pins them to my sides. He's right there, face so close to mine. Just as I think the eye contact is going to get awkward, Rhett releases my arms and envelopes me in an enormous hug. "Thank you," he whispers into my hair.

I savour the feeling of his arms around me, palms warm against my shoulders even through my shirt. I lift my hands, pressing them against his back and holding my friend close.

AFTER SCHOOL I meet Sophie beside her car.

She's leaning against the driver's side door listening to Theo, who's telling a story with more gestures than words, which is very Theo-like behaviour.

Theo spots me mid-story and abruptly stops talking. They give me a look; something like 'Sort yourself out before you lose her, you idiot', or maybe it's just a simple 'Hey'. Then they lean in and give Sophie a quick squeeze, whispering in her ear.

Theo gives me a big wave and a smirk, then disappears into the crowd of students filling the pathways between school and the carpark.

Sophie turns to greet me as I approach. My steps slow as I do. She was friendly and sweet and understanding in the library this morning, but I'm not sure I trust it.

I trust her completely. But I'm not sure I trust my judgement of what happened there.

But is there any way I could have misconstrued that hug?

She said we were friends. I didn't imply that. She did.

And the hug. I could receive a billion different hugs over my lifetime, but that hug … nothing's going to compare. It was top tier.

A little glow lights in my stomach as I remember her smiling up at me as she punched me in the arm. I'm pretty sure it hurt her hand more than my bicep, but it didn't stop her doing it again. The way she laughed, so light and free.

Then my clumsy attempt at pinning her arms to stop her from hurting her hand punching me again somehow evolved into that hug. My arms went around her before I realised how awkward it all was. I was about to pull away when she lifted her hands and pressed them into my back, turning her face and resting it against my neck.

It was a friendly hug … but at the same time it wasn't.

I need to talk everything through with her. I need to lay it all out on the table so she knows I'm not pulling back to hurt her, or because I don't like her.

I adore her.

She's beautiful. In fact, the word beautiful doesn't even encompass Sophie. It's not enough. Especially not when you consider who she is as a person, alongside her choppy pink haircut and deep brown eyes.

Today she's wearing jeans, as usual, but they look different. I wonder if they're new. They're distressed—not torn to shreds like some of the jeans girls wear, but they look worn in, except too shiny for it to be real wear and tear. She's paired them with an oversized shirt that's a soft purple. The sleeves are rolled, only a few of the buttons done up and it's slouchy and shows off way too much of her collarbone.

I mean, who knew a collarbone could be so sexy?

It reminds me of Saturday in the pool when I also saw a lot of her collarbones and a violet bra strap.

"Hey," I say.

She smiles. "Here, before I forget." She pulls the towel and jacket from her back seat and presses them into my hands. Skin to skin contact occurs and little tingles of electricity shoot up my arms. She slides her hands out from under mine and leaves me holding the bundle of fabric.

"Thanks," I say, trying desperately to think of something else to add.

I'm about to tuck the bundle under my arm when Sophie's hand lands on top of mine. I glance down at her and see hesitation in her eyes.

"Theo told me about the jacket," she says, and a rock appears in my throat. "That it was Dusty's."

I nod, the rock effectively blocking my throat and preventing any words from happening.

"I'm sorry if me wearing it was the wrong thing to do. I'm sorry if it upset you."

She's so sincere. She's so sweet and generous and good.

I shake my head. "No," I manage to croak. "It didn't upset me. I was … surprised, I guess. I wasn't expecting to see you standing there wearing it."

"I'm sorry I surprised you, then." She says it with one of those shy smiles of hers and I want to do way more than wrap her in a hug.

"Don't ever apologise for that," I say. "I love it when you surprise me."

She blushes. Hard. I love that almost more than when she surprises me.

"Dusty would have loved you," I say, and my voice catches on the last word. My eyes burn as tears begin to well. He truly would have adored Sophie. He'd have sat with her and talked about books for hours at a time. I could imagine them lying in the shade beside the pool talking for hours and mocking me relentlessly.

"Do you wanna go somewhere else?" Sophie's voice is soft, but it draws me back to the present.

"Yeah, that's probably a good idea," I say as I wipe at my face, removing a stray tear.

"We can do some pick-ups and then you won't get in trouble with your grandma. I'll cover for you."

This makes me chuckle. "What happened to the girl who blackmailed me with threats of telling on me to my grandma, huh?"

Sophie blushes again. "I wouldn't have actually done it," she murmured. "Now, come on. I'm driving today."

We climb into her car, me shoving the towel and jacket into her back seat again along with my backpack.

Sophie pulls out onto the street, the low hum of the radio the only sound.

"Is there anywhere in particular you want to do this?" she asks.

I assume she means me telling her about Dusty and Renee and all the other chaos that goes on inside my head. All the grief and pain and loss.

"We don't have to do this," I say.

"I know we don't have to, but if you still want to tell me, then I want to listen." She's quiet for a few beats. "You don't have to do this alone. I'm here for you."

"Then we're going to need some donuts, and there's a really cool place I'd like to show you. This time I promise I won't be a jerk."

She huffs out a little laugh. "Perfect. I was hoping I'd get a donut out of this." She flashes me a grin, then focusses on her driving.

I laugh then lean back in the seat, fighting the urge to reach over and hold her hand.

RHETT BUYS ME ANOTHER DONUT.

I could get used to this lifestyle.

As we're leaving the store I pull the door open and walk straight into Sam on his way into work.

"I'm so sorry," I gasp, trying to regain my breath after the fright of colliding with him.

"Hey, Sophie. No worries. I didn't see you either." He smiles at me, his eyes crinkling in the corners. He glances up and his smile falters as he spots Rhett, but quickly returns to normal. "You got everything you need?"

"We sure did," I say, pointing to the box of books Rhett is holding and lifting the bags of donuts up to show Sam.

"Awesome. I'd better get to it, but good to see you."

"Yeah, you too," I say, as he steps around me.

"I really like your hair," he calls before the door closes behind me.

I smile. I keep forgetting about it, even though I've had so many compliments on it today. A fair number of people seemed shocked I'd do something so drastic. Not that a few pink strands of hair feels reckless anymore. Not like it did before Friday. Now it feels right.

Yesterday, in honour of my new haircut, Theo took me shopping. I'd been nervous about my new outfit, even if it was only jeans and a shirt, but again, it felt exactly right. Like this is the real me, not the perfectly prim and proper girl everyone's always seen me as. I mean, I'm still that … now with a little bit of an edge. It's a feeling I hadn't expected to find through this stupid list thing I started with Rhett, but I have. And I love it.

Rhett and I head down the street towards my car. The parking this afternoon was awful and we're almost two blocks away, but Rhett insisted donuts were still required.

As we walk, I think about Sam and the way his smile slipped when he saw Rhett.

"Why doesn't Sam like you?" I ask, then realise that wasn't exactly the nicest way to say it. "I mean … I dunno." I shrug. "Do you guys have history or something?"

Rhett laughs like I've said something hysterically funny. "Sweetheart, he likes *you*. He's jealous because I'm spending time with you and you're never anything more than friendly and polite to him."

Huh? Say what? Sam? The thought had never crossed my mind. Sam likes me? I feel like that should give me a little thrill or something, but it doesn't. Not like the one I get when I think of Rhett.

Sam liking me doesn't exactly explain the issue he has with Rhett either. It's not like there's anything going on there. I'm pretty sure today is all about Rhett telling me we can never be anything more than friends. Also, no one but Theo knows anything about how I actually feel about Rhett, so there's no way Sam could be bothered by that. Surely.

"Well, he's got good taste," I joke feebly, trying to shift the awkward tension I'm suddenly feeling across my shoulders.

Rhett laughs again and reaches over to tug a lock my hair. "He sure does."

My face floods with heat and I press a hand against my cheek, hoping it hasn't turned fire engine red. He has to know what saying things like that does to me.

"Why don't you ask him out?"

"What?" I stop abruptly and Rhett walks three more steps before realising I'm no longer beside him. He shrugs.

"He's a nice guy, isn't he? No one seems to hate him, from what I've heard anyway. He'd hook you up with limitless donuts."

"I'm not sure that's a legitimate reason to date someone."

"Come on," he says. "If you won't do it for yourself, do it for me."

"Me date a guy so you can have access to donuts?"

"Yeah, sure," he says.

"Because that's not weird or mean at all," I say, rolling my eyes.

Rhett laughs, and I add this moment to my mental list of all the times I've made Rhett look this way—like he's truly happy and carefree, his eyes flashing silver and the corners of his mouth tipped up.

"But seriously, you could."

"Could what?"

"Go out with Sam," he says. "He could help you with that thing on your list."

Again, I berate myself for leaving the kiss on the list. Rhett doesn't need to know I haven't kissed anyone yet. I do not need him wing-manning me right now.

"I'll take your recommendation under advisement, but don't hold your breath."

"All right," Rhett says, and I might be imagining it, but he looks relieved at my answer.

I'm definitely imagining it. I have to be.

We climb into my car, and I head for the lookout. Rhett doesn't need to tell me any more about where he wants to go.

It's Monday afternoon, straight after school, so there's plenty of parking available.

We slip into the shade of the big tree, step over the fence and head along the trail.

This time I'm not nearly as apprehensive. I know Rhett better, and I've told Tonya we'll be at the warehouse later so I don't feel like I'm shirking my responsibilities.

Right now my only responsibility is being a good friend.

Rhett heads straight for the edge and lowers himself down, his legs hanging over the side.

I never thought I was afraid of heights, but maybe this secret little lookout spot is going to make me realise it.

My steps slow right down and I shuffle slightly closer.

"It's not a huge drop," Rhett says. "There's a paddock down there; it doesn't plunge straight to the ocean or anything."

Hearing that makes it a little easier to move forwards.

I take several deep breaths and turn my face up to the sun for a moment, grounding myself. The breeze is fresh and salty but has the first tinges of warmth to it—a hint of what's to come this summer. The sky is a cloudless blue, stretching on and on until it merges in a hazy line with the darker blue of the ocean.

I look back to Rhett, who's twisted back to reach out a hand towards me.

He's not goading me this time. He's not pushing. He's simply waiting for me, and I know that if I can't go through with this, he won't be mad. He'll move back towards me and we'll have this conversation sitting under one of the trees.

But I know that isn't what Rhett wants. He wants to tell me his story while sitting on the edge, his legs dangling over the side.

I take a couple of steps closer and reach my hand out for his. Our fingertips brush.

Another step and his fingers slide between mine.

"I've got you, sweetheart. I won't let you fall," he says, his eyes locked on mine.

It's too late, I think. Way too late. I've already fallen.

I HOLD my breath as Sophie slides her hand into mine.

She makes it to the edge and peeks over, her breath leaving her in a whoosh. But she stays, lowering herself to the ground beside me.

I've positioned it so she's next to the rock I usually lean against, thinking that will help her feel more grounded and less exposed.

She takes a few shaky breaths, and I can feel her quivering next to me. I grip her hand, trying to soothe her from this single point of contact.

She squeezes back and looks up at me. With her free hand she pushes her glasses up her nose.

"I'm good," she says.

"Yeah? You sure?"

She nods. "Yes." She looks around, taking in the view. "You're right about this spot. It was worth all my drama getting here."

I chuckle. "Are you afraid of heights? You should have said."

"I'm not scared of heights," she says. "Only falling off the edge of a cliff, apparently."

I laugh again. Laughing isn't totally foreign to me. It's happened a lot, even since Dusty's death. But when I'm laughing with Sophie it feels different. It feels like how it used to with him. Every time it's like the hole in my heart is patched a tiny bit. I don't expect that the hole will ever fully heal. It'll never be completely gone, but somehow Sophie makes it not quite as bad as before.

She sits beside me now, taking in everything around her, and silence falls between us.

"I don't even know where to start," I say eventually. "I feel like I kind of made this a big thing, but the reality is that it's not really." I sigh and focus on the point the ocean meets the sky. Sophie doesn't speak, but brushes her thumb against my hand.

"You already know about Dusty. I don't know what else to tell you about him. He was my best friend and now he's gone."

"I don't know very much about him. Could you tell me what he was like?" Her voice is soft, gentle. She's not demanding that I get on with telling her all the things that set me off on Saturday. She nudges me with her shoulder, but the brush is so light I don't know if it's an intentional move or not.

She wants to know what Dusty was like. I can do that. Dusty deserves for more people to know who he was. And I was telling the truth when I told Sophie that he would have adored her.

So I open my mouth and I tell her all about him.

I talk until my mouth feels dry. I tell Sophie all the greatest things about him. I tell her all the stupid things we did together. She laughs with me when I tell the funny stories, and she squeezes me hand even tighter when I tell her about the cancer.

I tell her about the diagnosis and Dusty's fight against it and how in the end, none of that mattered and he's gone.

By this point in the story she's leaning into me, her shoulder pressed against mine, our fingers clenched together.

I use my free hand to wipe the tears from my face, refusing to let go of Sophie's hand, even to hide the evidence of my grief. The whole point of this was to show her.

"I got so lost in losing him," I whisper. "I'm only beginning to realise how much. I didn't think about anyone else. I totally ditched Asher and Ellie. They needed me."

Sophie sniffs, and I realise she's also wiping tears away.

"I didn't mean to make you cry," I whisper, wanting to do whatever I have to so she never has to cry again.

"You didn't," she says. "It's the situation in general. You coped the best you could. Asher and Ellie will understand. Maybe not right now, but once they're older they'll understand."

"Maybe. The worst part, though, is someone told me. And I didn't listen."

"Who told you?"

I take a deep breath. Somehow this part feels worse than telling her about Dusty. "My ex-girlfriend."

Sophie flinches the tiniest bit at my words, like she's bothered by them. A part of me lights up at the thought she might be jealous. Another part of me tamps that down in a second, because I'm here to tell Sophie this part, the hard part. This is what we've been leading up to.

"Renee broke up with me about four months after Dusty died," I say eventually, when I've managed to get my emotions back under control.

"Wait," Sophie interrupts, holding up a hand. "She dumped you after your best friend died?" There's a fiery indignation burning in her eyes.

"Yeah, but she'd tried. She'd tried everything. I wouldn't listen. I treated her awfully. It wasn't on purpose, but I couldn't be there for her anymore, not like you're supposed to be in a relationship. She fought for me as long as she could. Then I guess the resentment took over."

Sophie shakes her head. "She should have kept trying."

I shrug. "I'm okay with it."

"You're not, though. Whatever she did or said, it hasn't left you, has it?"

Well, she's got me there.

"No, not all of it. I meant I'm okay with her dumping me. As for what she said, it would be a whole lot easier to move on from it if it wasn't true." I twist myself on the ledge, so instead of facing out towards the sea I'm facing Sophie directly. "She was right about so many things, but I'm only beginning to realise how much of it was truth. I'm still so messed up. I guess I hide it well, because most people don't even know about Dusty, let alone the rest of it." I take a shuddering breath. "But you know, Sophie. I want you to know, because I want you to know that when I react badly, it's not your fault. It's very likely nothing to do with you.

"I need to learn how to be a good friend again. I need to do that first, before ... well, before anything else, really. I know it's asking for a lot, asking for you to put up with my freak outs and moods and everything. You deserve so much better, but with you, for the first time since Dusty, I feel like maybe I'm not screwing everything up."

"You're not screwing anything up. The exact opposite," she whispers, and I almost don't catch the words as a gust of wind whips between us.

"You deserve the absolute best things," I say. "But right now all I can offer you is the truth, and a promise that I'll do my very best for you."

She doesn't say anything. I don't know if that's a good thing or not. Is she going to accept me as I am, or is she going to call me a weirdo and push me off the cliff?

Since she's Sophie, she doesn't push me off the cliff.

She opens her arms and pulls me into them, holding my head against her shoulder as I fail in my fight against the tears.

The tears of grief.

And tears of relief.

IN THE DAYS following Rhett's storytelling, we settle into the friendliest friendship ever. It's like we're both trying to prove we make good friends and nothing else.

Well, maybe that thought only occurs to me. Sometimes I think Rhett's trying to convince himself to stay, rather than dipping out on me.

After Rhett finished talking and he fell into my arms for the most heartbreaking hug I've ever been a part of, we scoffed our donuts down like they were going to fill the emotional void we'd just opened. Then we went on our rounds to collect more books and deliver them to the warehouse.

We've settled into an easy rhythm at school and the warehouse. Rhett waves when he's passing, he catches up to me between classes to say hello, and after school we sit together and sort books.

It's all very platonic.

Except for those occasional—or not so occasional—times when I realise how beautiful Rhett is to look at, or when our skin touches and the world spins around me. That happens a lot, since Rhett is such a touchy person. He's always slinging his arm around my shoulders or ruffling my hair, and he sometimes even throws in a nose boop.

When he arrives in the library on Thursday at lunchtime, he grins at me and saunters over, so cool and put together. His eyes flick over me then come to rest on my hair. I've braided the front sections back today and pinned them. I love it, but it feels so very different to anything I've ever done before. I'm wearing my new jeans again and an imitation leather jacket that I've "borrowed" from Mum's wardrobe. I've always coveted this jacket. I love the way it changed my whole outfit from jeans and a t-shirt to something that feels edgy and maybe even a little bit cool.

"I like your hair," Rhett says, reaching out and trailing his fingers along one of the plaits. "It's really pretty."

I try really hard not to, but I blush. "I like yours, too," I say. "You've really pushed the boundaries with it today."

He laughs so loudly the staff librarian pokes her head out of her office behind us. "Sorry," Rhett whispers to her. She gives him a stern look and withdraws.

We look at each other and burst into giggles, trying desperately to keep the volume down.

"I also like your sass," Rhett says eventually. "It suits you."

I scoff. There's no sass here. It's not something I could ever pull off. Unfortunately, my cheeks also flush some more, as they do every time Rhett compliments me.

"How can I help today?" I ask, in my primmest voice.

"Returning this, please," he says, sliding the book across the table.

"You know you can put it in the slot outside the door?"

"Yeah, but then I don't get to come and be sassed by the cute librarian."

My face flames. It could well be on fire by this point.

"Sorry," he mutters. "Sometimes I forget … You make it easy

to." He starts retreating, leaving the paperback on the counter, his hands sliding away from it as he steps back.

I reach out and snatch one of them up. I squeeze his hand. I don't say anything but when his eyes meet mine I give him a small smile. He exhales and halts his retreat.

"What are you going to read next?" I ask him, tapping the cover of the book he's returning.

He shrugs. "I'm not sure. I might start again?"

"You know there're hundreds of books in this library you could read?" I gesture around. "I mean yes, Percy is an excellent choice, and I'm all for rereading favourite books … but there's more you could be reading."

He shrugs again and looks decidedly uncomfortable. "I don't really read," he says.

"You read this whole series in what? Two weeks?"

"I don't really read. Besides these," he corrects himself.

"Why?" I blink at him, stunned. I kind of assumed Rhett was a hidden bookworm. That he loved to read but didn't want anyone to know about it. Which I'll never understand. Of all the things to be embarrassed by, why would reading be one of them?

He takes a deep breath and exhales slowly. "They were Dusty's favourite," he says eventually, and it's one of the exceptionally rare times I detect a hint of a blush on his cheeks.

Ah. That makes sense. A lot of sense.

Still, there're so many amazing stories in the world, it seems sad to let Rhett keep reading the same ones on repeat forever.

"Come with me," I say, gesturing for him to follow as I head into the stacks. I come to a stop in the R section. "Have you read the next series? Same world, some of the same characters, plus some new ones?"

Rhett shakes his head, looking a little dumbfounded. "I didn't know there were more. Just those first five."

"Oh, there's more," I say, pointing to a row of books and trailing my finger along the spines. "Here. Try these … if you want." I pull a couple of books from the shelf and hand them over. "You can also take out more than one book at a time," I say.

"Yeah, but if I only take one then I have to come and see this funny librarian girl more often. You know, I think at this point we might even be friends."

"Ha, so funny," I say as I roll my eyes.

I check out the books for Rhett, and with a wave, smile and promise to see me after school, he disappears through the library doors.

I immediately pull out my phone, even though I definitely should not be using it in the library.

I open a new email message and type in the address for my favourite bookstore in town. I hurriedly tap out the email and hit send.

When I get to the warehouse that afternoon, arriving before Rhett, I head straight to the corner where we've been stacking the children's books. I pull out the box set Tonya offered me two weeks ago and put it aside with the box of books I'm buying from the book fair.

33 /
rhett

BEING friends with Sophie is so much fun.

We're doing nothing out of the ordinary, but I'm having the most fun I've had in years. Now that we've got past Sophie's shyness and my messed-up weirdness, we've settled into this comfortable space that involves a lot of me going out of my way to say hello to her, and a lot of her either blushing or rolling her eyes at me.

The moment the bell rang at the end of lunchtime on Thursday, I remembered I'd forgotten to ask Sophie something, so I stake out her car at the end of the day.

Before too long she and Theo appear, Theo howling with laughter at something Sophie is saying.

"Oh, you're brutal," Theo says between gasps of laughter. "I love it when you're sassy."

"I'm not sassy," Sophie says. "You're so weird. Hey, Rhett."

"You are so sassy." Theo turns to me. "Back me up?"

I glance at Sophie, who's staring me down. "You're a little sassy," I say with a shrug, and grin as she rolls her eyes.

"Remind me why I'm friends with either of you again?"

"Because I'm delightful," says Theo. "Him … I'm not so sure. I think you might just be doing it for the street cred. Anyway, I gotta run. See ya." They blow a kiss to Sophie and wave in my direction, then race across the carpark.

"Oof, only being my friend for the street cred, huh? You *are* brutal."

"Oh, like you've got any kind of reputation that's going to benefit me. How's your day been?"

This is something I love about Sophie. She always asks and she always seems to actually be interested in my answer.

"Yeah, it was all right." I shrug. It's school, there isn't much else to report. "Hey, I forgot to ask earlier, I'm taking Asher and Ellie bowling this weekend. Saturday afternoon. Do you want to come?"

"You sure you want me there?"

I frown at her question. "What do you mean? Why wouldn't I want you there?"

She shrugs and looks at me thoughtfully. "I don't want to intrude on your time with them."

I can't help myself and reach out, wrapping an arm around her shoulders and pulling her into my side for a quick hug. I squeeze her tight and let her go. She blinks up at me in confusion, like she does most of the times I'm affectionate with her.

"You won't be intruding. Plus, it's on the list."

The mention of the list always gets a reaction out of Sophie. Sometimes she blushes, sometimes she rolls her eyes, sometimes she groans and covers her face with her hands, which is what she does now.

"That stupid list," she mutters. "I can't believe I did that."

I take hold of her wrists and gently lower her hands away from her face. She tilts her chin to look up at me and I smile. "I'm so, so glad you did, sweetheart."

She stares at me, eyes wide, lips parted slightly, like she's in shock. It's an expression I'm getting used to seeing.

I know what it means, but touching her comes so naturally I don't think about it until after I've done it and made her look at me like this. Like she wants more.

I remind myself, again, of all the reasons it's a bad idea. "I'd better go," I say. "I won't be there this afternoon, so I'll see you tomorrow. Think about Saturday."

She nods and lifts a hand to wave, but doesn't say anything. I turn and head towards my own car, pausing on the way when Ricky calls out to me.

"What's up with you and Sophie?" he asks when I get close enough so he doesn't have to shout anymore. Brad and Evan break off their conversation to hear my answer.

I shrug, trying for nonchalant. I've been waiting for this moment. When I have to explain this friendship I have with Sophie, when my friends have no idea about my grandparent-ordered reparations, or why I even need to make reparations in the first place.

They know my friend died last year. They know Renee broke up with me, but they don't know why. They've no doubt noticed I've been withdrawing more and more as time has gone on.

"We're friends," I say. "She's cool."

"That's it?" Evan asks.

"That's all it is," I say, immediately defensive.

He waves his hands, telling me to settle down. "What I mean is, is that all you're going to tell us about her? Are we not worth your time anymore?"

"What? She's ... Are you bothered because I'm friends with her?" I don't like where this conversation is going. It's making heat prickle at the back of my neck and my fingers curl into fists.

"I'm not bothered that you're friends with her. Frankly, I think you need some more friends." He lets out a heavy breath. "You know what, don't worry about it. Forget I said anything."

But I won't forget, and I will worry about it. I've never been as close with Ricky, Evan and Brad as I was with Dusty, but that doesn't mean they haven't been awesome friends to me for years, even in the worst of the grief when I was barely conscious enough to function.

Evan turns away, but I grab his shoulder and turn him back to me.

"Sorry," I say. I take a breath and think about how it felt to be honest with Sophie. I don't want to unload on my friends, but I could tell them some of it. "My grandparents are making me help sort books for this charity book fair thing."

"Oh, yeah, I've seen the signs for it," Brad says, like it's no big deal. I guess it probably isn't except for in my head, where it felt like the worst punishment in the world and something I should be embarrassed by.

"Well, Sophie is helping too. So we've been hanging out a bit. Once you get past the quiet she's really funny, and she's genuinely nice."

"Hot, too," Ricky puts in.

"It's not like that," I say, giving him a shove.

He studies me for a moment. "I'll withhold judgement. But dude, we're not mad you've got other friends. Just remember that we're your friends too, okay?"

He whacks me on the shoulder with so much enthusiasm it actually hurts, but I understand the sentiment.

"Yeah, I'll remember."

IT'S strange that Rhett isn't here this afternoon.

I'm so used to him being here, sorting books next to me and joking about how good or bad a book might be.

Unfortunately, the ones he seems to have the most fun mocking are the ones I love the most. Occasionally I join in the mocking and judging, his humour impossible to ignore, but when it's a book I adore and he holds it up for my opinion, I've taken to removing it gently from his grip and placing it on its appropriate pile while he mutters "another one" in bewilderment, as though a person shouldn't have several dozen favourite books.

But this afternoon Rhett isn't here, so I'm mindlessly sorting books on my own.

Tonya slides into a seat beside me and picks up a hardback that looks like a thriller or something else I'm unlikely to read. "I can see the light," she says.

"What's that, Flynn Ryder?"

She squints at me and I wave off my movie reference.

"At the end of the tunnel."

"Oh, right." I glance over at the end of the warehouse where we started with a huge stack of boxes. Slowly we've been whittling it down. Soon we'll have all the books sorted into their respective categories and it'll be time to start pricing them. The thought of pricing thousands of books isn't overwhelming at all.

"You've been so much help," she says. "And Rhett, too. Where is he today?"

I shrug. "I dunno. He never said, only that he wouldn't be here."

"Suppose the boy's entitled to some kind of life," she says, then laughs. "You are too, you know."

I roll my eyes. "Yes, I do know. I'm happy with my life."

"Good." She sorts a few books from my pile. "I really like your hair, as you know." I nod, remembering her gushing compliments on Saturday when she first saw it. "What brought it on?"

"What brought what on? Me getting my hair cut and coloured?"

"Yeah, don't get me wrong, it's great. It's, well ... it was surprising, I guess."

I laugh. "Yeah, maybe. There're a lot of things I want to do; things that would probably surprise you. I guess I needed some confidence to start doing them."

She gives me a look that's hard to describe, but I know where she's going next.

"Does the lovely Rhett have something to do with all this?"

I really don't want to blush right now, because she'll tease me relentlessly. Unfortunately I've never had any luck controlling my blushing, so with flaming cheeks I roll my eyes and say, "I'm not sure lovely is the word I'd use to describe him."

Tonya laughs. "No, maybe not. But answer the question, Soph."

"In a way—not the way you think—yeah, he's got something to do with it."

"What do you mean 'not the way I think'?" she asks.

"We're friends," I say. "Nothing else."

She snorts, then apologises. "Sorry, honey, you're going to have to try harder to make me believe that one."

I sigh and slump forward until my forehead rests against the table. "It's not my choice," I mutter. "I would really, really like to not be friends with him."

Tonya rubs circles on my back, like she has since I was little. Heat fills my eyes and I blink back tears. I'm not going to cry over him.

I push myself upright and brush my hair back from my face, turning to face my aunt. "He's got some stuff going on and doesn't think he's in a good place for a relationship." I shrug. "It is what it is."

Tonya gives me a gentle smile. "At least he had the decency to tell you, to be upfront about it."

"Yeah." I smile back, but it feels a little wobbly.

"Doesn't mean it doesn't hurt though, right?"

I nod, incapable of words at this point.

She pats my hand, my back out of reach now I'm upright again. "You guys will figure it out, if it's meant to happen."

"Yeah, I'm not sure it is meant to happen though. Which is sad, but it is what it is, I guess. But I'm lucky that I still get to be his friend."

"And he's very lucky to have you." She pauses and rearranges some books. "Now, backtracking a little, what are these things you want to do that would surprise me? Please share."

I laugh. She's so excited. So I tell her a few things off the list, though I don't actually reference the list they're on, or the worn piece of paper with flower doodles down the sides that I'd written them on and given to Rhett Carmichael, of all people.

I tell her about the undying longing to dye my hair, and how good it feels, how much it feels like me despite my mother's reservations. She scoffs at that, telling me my mum needs to lighten up.

I tell her about how I want to go to a concert for the first time ever and feel the bass of real instruments vibrating through my feet, the heat of the crowd around me as we sing along to the lyrics together.

I tell her about how I want to learn to dance and that I don't care what genre, as long as it's not too uptight. I want to be in my body, and learn how to make it move. I want the confidence to dance, not necessarily on stage, but anywhere. I want to know that I can, and that I wouldn't look like a complete fool while doing it.

And then I tell her about the thing on my list that seems the most out of reach at this point, aside from a first kiss with a guy I like. I push the thought of kissing Rhett away for the millionth time today, and tell Tonya about this other item, the one I've planned in intricate detail—right up to actually going through with it.

"If you want to do it, I can help you," she says, a devilish glint in her eye that she does not share with her sister, my mother. "Shall we?"

"Yes," I say. "Definitely."

"WHERE WERE YOU THIS AFTERNOON?" Grandad asks when I sit down at the dinner table.

I glance at Grandma, who sends me a supportive look.

"I had an appointment," I mutter. I don't want to get into it right now. I'm exhausted

"An appointment?"

"Yeah," I say. "Grandma knew about it."

"And what was the appointment about?"

I don't understand why he's being so harsh about it. Does he think I was shirking my duties? I guess he probably doesn't realise I'd happily be at the book warehouse so long as Sophie was there with me. And since she's helping because she wants to, she's usually there.

Grandad raises his eyebrows at me, staring me down across the table.

"It was a doctor's appointment," I snap. It's close to the truth; close enough that I don't feel like I'm lying to him.

Grandad harrumphs. "Make sure you're there on Saturday. You've got some time to make up what with today and Monday."

I freeze with my fork halfway to my mouth. It's quivering,

which can only mean my hands are shaking. I try to speak, but even after clearing my throat I can't make words form. He can't force me to go down there, can he? I can't go. I can't bail on Ellie and Asher.

Also, wait, Monday? How does he know about Monday?

"Monday?" I croak.

"Yeah, I heard you were AWOL."

I glance at Grandma and she flinches a little. Did she dob me in? She lifts one shoulder in a shrug. Maybe it wasn't her.

"I was with Sophie; we were picking up books."

Grandad stares me down, but Grandma comes in to bat for me. "Yes, that's right. I remember you bringing them in." She turns to Grandad. "Where did you hear he wasn't helping on Monday?"

Grandad looks a little flustered. "I saw Trevor earlier, when I was refuelling my car. He mentioned he hadn't seen much of Rhett this week."

I roll my eyes. Trevor was a pain in the backside, for everyone.

Grandma scoffs. "That man's an idiot."

"Still," Grandad says, "the fair is getting closer. You'll need more help. Rhett can put in a few extra hours." I bet he thinks I'm lying about today.

I'm disappointed. I thought things had been going well, especially since last weekend when I mowed the lawns for him

"I can't," I say, before I've properly thought out how to broach the subject.

Grandad turns his attention back to me.

"I can go in the morning on Saturday, but not the afternoon. I have to be finished by one."

"And when were you planning on telling us this?"

"Um, now?" I hadn't realised I was supposed to tell them every little detail. Sure, they'd given me a curfew that was way earlier than the one Mum gave me, but I didn't realise I had to run every excursion past them. I hadn't last weekend.

"What's so important that you have to skip out on helping your grandmother?"

Honestly, he's making it sound like I'm the worst kind of delinquent and that Grandma cannot possibly cope without my dedicated attention.

"I'm …" I think for a moment about the best way to phrase it. "I'm babysitting."

Ellie will kill me if she finds out I referred to us hanging out as babysitting. And it's not like I'm doing it because Aimee needs me to watch the kids while she does something else. I messaged her this morning, asking if Ellie and Asher would want to hang out this weekend. She said they were free Saturday afternoon and had been asking about going bowling. So I offered to take them.

Because I've missed them. I just didn't realise how much until I saw them again, and I know if I tell Grandad I'm "hanging out" with them, he'll think I only want to avoid having to help.

"You're babysitting?"

Yeah, okay, so me babysitting is a pretty unlikely scenario. "Yeah, for Asher and Ellie."

"Dustin's brother and sister?" Grandad asks, and I can tell he's wavering.

"Yeah. I said I'd hang out with them on Saturday afternoon. Please don't make me cancel." The emotion in my voice surprises me. It clearly surprises Grandad.

"You don't have to cancel," he says gruffly. We eat in silence for a minute, two. With a sigh, he sets down his cutlery. "I'm not trying to be your jailor, Rhett," he says. "We've been worried about you and we're trying to look out for you."

I nod. It's stiff and jerky. "I know that." My voice feels rough and my eyes start to burn. "I didn't mean to cause all this trouble," I say, my voice now only capable of a low whisper.

Suddenly, in one breath, it all becomes too much. I push back from the table.

"Can I—I need to … sorry," I mutter, then rush from the room. There's dead silence behind me. I can imagine my grandparents staring across the table at each other, twin looks of shock on their faces. I'm not usually the kind of guy who runs from a room crying. I'm the kind of guy who buries emotions, makes jokes and smiles at everyone.

I head for my room, but it's too quiet. It doesn't smother the sounds tearing from my body. Instead I burst into the bathroom and turn the shower to scalding hot. When I step in I hiss at the heat, but soon I'm immune to it.

I lean against the wall as sobbing overtakes me. I can't think straight. I can't think about the good things.

I'm swallowed by the grief of losing Dusty. The loss grips me.

Then the other memories start to crowd in.

Renee breaking up with me, calling me self-centred, telling me I was no fun anymore and I only thought of myself. That she couldn't put up with my behaviour anymore, that she wanted someone who cared about her. I hate her for what she did. But she was also right.

An image of Ellie flashes into my mind, of the last time I saw her before the arcade. She was at the cemetery, her face streaked with tears as she knelt beside Dusty's grave. I don't think she ever saw me.

That was the day I really screwed everything up.

I didn't mean to. I didn't mean to start the fire. I didn't mean to cause any damage.

I didn't mean to make everyone lose what little faith they had left in me.

36 /
sophie

RHETT SEEMS DISTANT TODAY.

He was distant yesterday too, but that was because I didn't see him, not once. I don't even know if he was at school.

Today he looks tired as he carries boxes back and forth across the warehouse. I catch his grandma watching him, a small, concerned frown on her face.

He waved when he first arrived but didn't come over to talk to me. I haven't yet found a legitimate excuse for getting up so I can make our paths cross. I suppose I could say I'm going to the bathroom, but maybe I'm a little scared that there's more going on here and he doesn't want to talk to me.

Which is a ridiculous thought, because we've spent so much time this past week talking and clearing the air. We know exactly where we stand with each other.

Plus, I'm his friend and I shouldn't shy away when I'm worried about him. I can tell by his grandma's face she's worried too.

I debate with myself for another ten minutes, and right as I'm about to pick up a box of books to move, Rhett appears by my side.

"Want me to take that one?" he asks. There's a small smile on his lips, but it doesn't reach the rest of his face.

I study him. He looks even more exhausted up close. His eyes are red with dark smudges under them, and he could have done with a shave. I've never seen him with this much stubble and I hate that I think it makes him even hotter, especially when it's obvious he just couldn't be bothered dealing with it.

"Yeah, that'd be good, thanks," I say, and he goes to slide the box off the table into his arms. I grab hold of his wrist. "Wait."

He stops, leaves the box sitting on the table and watches me warily.

"Are you okay?"

"Yeah," he says. "Well, I will be, I guess." He says it like a question, like he's asking me if he'll be okay.

"Let's take a little break," I say, sliding my hand down so it fits inside his. I lead him out of the warehouse and around the back, where there's a strip of grass before an area of bush springs up from nowhere. It's a welcome reprieve in this industrial area of town.

I lean against the warehouse wall and Rhett does the same, then he slides down the wall so he's sitting scrunched up on the ground. I lower myself down beside him.

"What's going on?" I say, my voice soft like I'm talking to a startled animal or upset child.

He shrugs. "The usual. It's ... it's a lot right now."

"Yeah, it is," I agree, then slide an arm across his shoulders and pull his head down to rest against my shoulder.

"I had a doctor's appointment on Thursday," he whispers. "They're recommending counselling."

I'm surprised he's telling me about it, but I try not to show it.

"Are you going to go?" I ask. "Though you don't have to tell me if you don't want to."

He sighs and readjusts himself so he's more comfortable. I try not to think how perfectly he fits next to me. "Sweetheart, I want to tell you everything."

He doesn't say anything after that, which I find a little funny, but I don't mention it. I sit with him in silence, my fingers smoothing his hair.

If I think about that too much—my fingers being in his hair, his head pressed against my shoulder—my head starts to spin, so I look at the trees and listen to the birds chirping.

Eventually he sits up and turns red-rimmed eyes to me. "I'm—"

"Don't say you're sorry, Rhett."

He snaps his mouth closed. "Okay then, I won't," he says, a little bit of the surly Rhett I first met peeking through. But it doesn't intimidate me now. Not now I know him.

"Good. There's nothing to apologise for." I reach up and push his hair away from his eyes. "Did you get my message about bowling?"

He nods. "You don't have to come, though. I know I'm not much fun."

"Mmm, yes. You're the least fun person I've ever met. I never have fun with you." I smile, obviously joking.

He flinches and drops his eyes.

"Hey." I run my fingers along his jaw and tilt his chin up so he has to look at me, like he's done so many times to me. "That's what she said, isn't it?"

There's a long pause and I wonder if I broke everything, then slowly he nods. "Yeah," he says, and it's barely louder than a breath.

"She's wrong. Completely and totally wrong. I've had more fun with you than I have with anyone, ever. If you want me to come with you this afternoon, then I'm there, okay?"

He nods. "I don't deserve you."

I stand and reach out a hand, helping to pull him to his feet. "Yeah, you do. Now, come on, we'd better get back to work so we can go do fun stuff later."

"Thank you," he says as he snakes an arm around my back and pulls me in for another of his utterly incredible hugs. I lean into him and inhale the smell of him. I'm so creepy and weird, but I can't help myself.

A noise behind me has me jerking away. I spin around to see Tonya standing at the corner of the building. She has both hands raised. "My bad. Pretend I'm not here."

Rhett laughs and it makes my own heart happy. "It's okay, Tonya. Sorry we bailed."

"Hey, you guys are here voluntarily. You don't have required work hours. If you want to hide round here and, ah, do whatever it is you're doing, who am I to stop you?" She laughs. "Although, your grandma was looking for you. I think maybe she was worried?"

"Yeah, probably. It's been a rough couple of days. I think I should go talk to her." He reaches down and squeezes my hand quickly before disappearing back around the corner of the building, leaving me with Tonya.

"Don't say a word," I say, holding up a hand.

"I didn't say anything."

"Good. Keep it that way."

She mimes zipping her lips, but sends me a grin so devilish I groan, then head back inside to my books.

I'M UNEXPECTEDLY nervous when I pull into the driveway to pick up Ellie and Asher.

Maybe it's the emotional turmoil of the past few days, seemingly triggered by my doctor's insistence I need extra support, or maybe it's simply that I know I really messed up when it comes to Ellie and Asher and I badly want them to forgive me.

Asher barges out the front door before I'm halfway up the path. "Rhett!" he cries as he slides to a stop beside me. I'm pretty sure he was going to hug me but stopped himself at the last minute, like he wasn't sure if that's okay anymore.

"Hey, buddy," I say, raising my hand for a high five. He slaps it, then I loop my arm over his shoulder and lead up him the rest of the way up the path. He immediately starts telling me about a dog he saw at the football field this morning.

I hesitate when I get to the front door. Do I knock? I don't know what the etiquette is now. I never used to knock. I'd barrel right in, shout a hello to Aimee and her husband Thomas and head straight for Dusty's room.

Asher saves me from my own dilemma when he barges inside, shouts "Rhett's here!" and drags me in after him.

Aimee leans against the doorway leading into the kitchen. "Hey, Rhett. Asher, go finish getting yourself ready." She turns her attention back to me. "You sure you want to do this? That boy does not stop. Ever."

I grin. "Yeah, of course I want to do this." I rub at the back of my neck. "I'm sorry it's taken me so long to get around to it."

Aimee waves me off. "We've all been dealing with it differently, Rhett. It's okay. We understand." She pushes off the wall and comes to stand in front of me, placing both hands on my shoulders. She has to tip her head back to look me in the eye. I don't know when that happened. Getting so tall that she has to look up to me. I've spent my whole life looking up to *her*.

"You don't need to apologise. You're always welcome here. Always. But we also understand if you don't want to be here."

I blink several times, really fast, and when the tears threatening to spill over are back under control, I nod. "Thanks, Aimee."

"Come on, Ellie." Asher's voice echoes down the hall, breaking the moment. "Rhett's here."

"I'm coming!" she shouts back. "I'll be out when I'm ready, and if you keep annoying me I'm going to take longer."

I laugh.

Aimee gives me a tired look. "Easy for you, blessed only child," she says, deadpan. "Come have a drink while you wait for her. She could take anywhere from a minute to twenty. It's like she enjoys keeping us guessing."

Ellie is ready to go in an entirely acceptable five minutes. We pile into my car and I pull into the street, heading towards Sophie's house.

"You guys remember my friend Sophie? Who I was with the other night?"

"Yeah," Ellie says.

"Uh-huh," Asher says, bouncing in the back seat. "Is she coming with us?"

"If it's okay with you guys, then yeah. But if you don't want her to come it's okay."

"Rhett, Mum already checked with us. We're fine with her coming. Besides, you can't uninvite her now. It's a little late for that," Ellie says with the most dramatic eye roll I've ever seen. She does have a point, though. When did Dusty's little sister grow up so much?

I pull to a stop outside Sophie's house, and before I have a chance to even get out and go to her front door, she comes through it. She waves and locks the door behind her then strides down the path, clutching the strap of her bag where it crosses her body.

She's wearing jeans and a white knitted sweater that slides off one shoulder. The front section of her hair is pinned back on each side of her head with sparkly clips.

She looks amazing. As usual.

Ellie slides out of the front seat and says hello to Sophie, who argues that she's fine sitting in the back. Ellie wins the argument and climbs into the back while Sophie slips into the seat next to me.

"Hey," I say, noticing her make-up now she's up close. I'm pretty sure she's even wearing eyeliner, complete with the little flicks out the sides. And lipstick. Shiny, pink lipstick that emphasises the shape of her mouth. She definitely wasn't wearing that earlier. I'm in one of those moments when the world falls away and all I can see is Sophie; when I notice how much effort she's put in. How much she's stolen the breath from my body.

Ellie groans from the back seat and I turn my head enough to see her slap her palm right across her face, shaking her head as she does. "I love your hair," she says, breaking the spell between me and Sophie. It's probably for the best. This kid knows what she's doing.

Sophie's cheeks turn pink as she pulls her gaze from mine and directs it towards Ellie. "Thanks. I really like it."

"Did your mum freak out?"

Sophie shrugs. "Not as bad as I was expecting. Maybe she's harbouring it all for another time when she can pull it out and use it against me."

"Ugh, that'd be right," Ellie groans.

"Oh, come on," I say. "Your mum's cool."

"My mum is fine. She's a mum. They're supposed to be fine. I will give her credit that other people think she's cool and not totally lame."

Sophie and I share a look and a smile. I can tell she's thinking the same thing as me—that Ellie isn't wrong. Somehow she's got real wise in the past year.

I kind of wish I could have had some of her wisdom. Maybe then I wouldn't have let things get so bad.

I MIGHT BE EVEN WORSE at bowling than I am at air hockey.

Even Asher is annihilating me.

"I give up," I groan as my ball falls into the gutter … again.

"Don't do that, sweetheart," Rhett says, wrapping an arm around me and pulling me into his side. "You can only go up from here."

"Well, it's impossible for me to suck any more than I already do."

Rhett laughs and turns his face into my hair for a brief second before letting me go and retrieving his ball, no doubt ready to score yet another strike.

"I thought she wasn't his girlfriend," I hear Asher whisper to Ellie behind me.

"She's not," Ellie whispers back. I keep my eyes locked on Rhett as he takes his turn.

"Well, that's not what it looks like," Asher says. "Didn't he kiss her hair? Do people usually kiss people's hair if they aren't girlfriend and boyfriend?"

"I dunno," Ellie says. "All I can say is, the fact she isn't his girlfriend makes him a total idiot."

Asher giggles.

Rhett doesn't score a strike. He gets a spare this turn. He spins and grins at me when the score flashes on the board.

"Show off," I grumble. I collapse onto the seat beside Ellie now she's finished her conversation with her brother about my relationship status.

"He's a jerk, right?" she says, but she's smiling fondly at Rhett clowning around with Asher.

"The biggest," I agree.

"Oh, come on sweetheart, I am not." Rhett flicks at my hair and I smack his hand away, but the touch lingers longer than it should when his fingers somehow tangle with mine. I suck in a breath and drop my hand to my lap.

This keeps happening. These tiny moments.

I don't know how to make them stop. I don't want them to stop, but I need them to. I need to go back to my little bubble inside the library, where the only person I had to worry about was Theo.

I need to go back to the time when my heart was safe.

But I can't.

Instead I'm here with a boy and no one is more surprised than me, except perhaps my mother.

"Why don't you invite Theo over here?" she asked yesterday when I asked if it was okay for me to hang out with a friend. "I haven't seen them in ages."

"Because I'm not seeing Theo tomorrow," I replied. "It's another friend."

She was so shocked I have another friend she sat there blinking at me for several long moments before finally responding with, "Oh. Okay, then. Yes, I suppose that's fine. Be safe, etcetera."

As if I'm not the most careful, safe person she knows.

It would be more amusing if it wasn't so depressing that before Rhett, I had a single friend.

But it's hard to make friends when the things they like to do and the places they like to hang out make you a panicky mess. I never trust their goodwill, either; like people wanting to hang out are setting me up to be the punchline to a joke.

It's all too hard, too complicated and way, way too stressful. So I stick to my books.

I pull myself back to the present when Asher yelps in delight at knocking down almost all the pins on his next turn.

Rhett high-fives him, shouting and hollering and making the kid feel like King of the World.

Ellie and I share a basket of fries and watch them.

"Why aren't you together?" Ellie asks abruptly.

"What?"

She rolls her eyes. She's so good at it I'm tempted to ask for lessons. "You and Rhett. Why aren't you dating? Or are you, and it's like some big secret?" She gasps. "Ooh, do your parents hate him and don't want you dating him? Is that it? Like a forbidden romance thing?"

"Woah, woah, woah." I hold my hands up. "What are you talking about?"

She blushes. "Sorry. I read this book and the girl's parents wouldn't let her date the guy she liked, so they had to have this whole secret romance. It was great."

I laugh. "It sounds amazing, but no, there's no secret romance." I sigh. "You'd better have your turn."

"Don't think this is getting you out of this conversation," she says, walking backwards towards the ball rack.

"Of course not," I say, hoping desperately that she gets distracted and I'm off the hook.

"Of course not what?" Rhett takes Ellie's place, shovelling fries into his mouth. Our shoulders press together like they're magnetised.

"Nothing, she's just being Ellie."

He grins. "I forgot how much of a little sister she is. I missed annoying her."

"Such a jerk, leave her alone." I shove him.

He drapes an arm across the back of the seat and turns to face me. "I think she missed it too?" he says, his expression turning unsure as his voice softens into a question.

"Yeah, I think you're right. Just this one time."

He chuckles.

"Do you want to hang out some more after you've dropped the kids home?" I say, and I catch my breath. I didn't mean to say the words. I was thinking them, I was thinking about how I'd really like to spend some more time with him, how I'd like to be alone with him. As much as I like Ellie and Asher, I want more of the Rhett I see when it's only us.

I think back over the list and how this whole thing started with Rhett telling me to live a little. I think of all the things I've done since that day and even how the smallest, most inconsequential things on the list, like going to an arcade, have altered my life. They've given me the confidence I needed. The confidence I need for this very moment.

"I want to show you something," I say.

Rhett's eyes darken. "Yeah, I think we could do that. What do you want to show me?"

"Boom! Beat that!" Ellie shouts and the moment fractures.

Which is probably a good thing, because I have no intention of telling Rhett what it is I want to show him. The whole point is that I *show* him.

I watch Rhett congratulate Ellie on her strike and they bust out a victory dance. It's obviously something from before … from when Dusty was still a part of this scene, because they both know all the moves. Asher tries to keep up but can't, and his disappointment is evident.

Ellie is laughing, staring up at Rhett like she would a big brother. Rhett promises to teach Asher the moves.

The moment is perfect. Whatever else happens—tonight, tomorrow, any time in the future—I'll always be grateful I had this moment with Rhett.

THERE'S a weird buzzing in my blood brought on by the neon lights and pounding music and the happiness this moment is giving me.

I grin up at Sophie as she puts yet another basket of fries on the table in front of me. She places a milkshake down beside it. Ellie adds two more.

"I'll be back in a minute," Sophie says, gesturing over her shoulder in the direction of the bathrooms. "Asher's over there." She points to where he's wistfully watching a group of kids play with one of those claw machines.

Ellie slides onto the bench beside me as Sophie weaves her way through the crowds. "She's really cool."

"Sophie? Yeah, she is."

"So, why aren't you dating her?"

I startle at her question and drop the fry I'm holding. It lands on the front of my t-shirt, splattering tomato sauce everywhere. "What?"

Ellie hands me a stack of serviettes with a bland expression on her face, like she isn't buying into me throwing food on myself as an excuse to get out of the conversation. Which is not at all what happened. Not at all.

She watches as I clean up my shirt as best I can. "Before … before Dusty," she says, and finally drops her gaze away from me, fiddling with the straw in her milkshake. She takes a deep breath. "You would have been all over it. You'd have flirted and charmed your way into being a part of her life."

"Who says I haven't done that already?"

She snorts. "Well, it's kind of obvious you have, but I mean, you wouldn't be holding back. If she was into it, she'd be your girlfriend."

"Yeah, well, have you considered that Sophie doesn't want to be my girlfriend?"

She laughs outright this time. "Yeah, and I'm a flying pig." She rolls her eyes and seriously, this girl could give lessons. She's a grand master. "She's so into you it's ridiculous."

"Ridiculous?" I echo.

"Yes, ridiculous. And weird. Doesn't she have any taste?"

I gently shove her shoulder. "Brutal, El. What happened to the sweet kid from a few years back?"

The smile drops off her face. "I guess I had to grow up."

"I'm so sorry, El," I say, stretching out my arm. She slides along the bench seat and turns her face into my shoulder as I wrap my arm around her. "I'm sorry about Dusty and I'm sorry I haven't been around much."

She sniffs. "I get it. I get why you haven't been."

"I got caught up in my own drama."

Ellie gives a wet laugh and sniffs again, pushing herself upright. "You always were super dramatic."

"Pfft, you can talk."

"Anyway," she says, drawing out the word. "Back to the point of this conversation." She slides her fingertips under her eyes, wiping away any traces of tears. "Since you no longer have Dusty to sort you out when you're being an idiot, I'm taking it upon myself."

"You say that like Dusty used to give me good advice."

"We all know Dusty used to give you good advice. I'm pretty sure it was him who always said you could do better than Renee."

"Oof, low blow, El. How do you even remember her?"

"I remember her because she was mean, and you've never been mean, so I didn't understand it. Sophie, though … *that* I understand."

"It's complicated," I say, kind of hating myself saying those words.

Ellie rolls her eyes yet again. "Idiot," she mutters. "Why's it complicated?"

"It just is."

"Don't be annoying. Tell me. I'm going to get it out of you eventually."

"Yeah? How are you going to do that?"

"I have my ways. But it'll be way easier for us both if you just tell me. What's holding you back?"

I sigh and rub at my hair. "I'm not right for her," I say. "It would be all wrong."

"You like her?"

"Yes, Ellie. I like her. A lot. A stupid amount. Okay? Are you happy?"

"Not in the slightest. If you like her, and she likes you, why are you not together? You call her sweetheart and you're constantly touching her in some way and she looks at you like she's in love with you."

"How would you even know what that looks like?"

"Because I do. I see things, Rhett. Now stop avoiding the point I'm making."

"Fine. I'm not with her because I'm trying to be a better person. I'm not right for her, and for me to convince her to be with me … I'd be so selfish to do that. I'm trying to be better than that."

"Okay, first of all, you don't have to convince her of anything. She likes you, you stupid idiot. And second, why do you think you're not right for her?"

"Because she's told me what she wants, and I'm not that person."

"How long ago did she tell you?"

"What?"

"You heard me. Geez, stop playing dumb and maybe we'll be able to finish this conversation today."

"We can finish it anytime, El."

"Not until you admit that you're being so, so stupid. She likes you. Whatever she told you before, maybe she changed her mind? Maybe she described you but you don't see yourself that way?

"The only way you're being selfish right now is not giving you guys a shot. You could be happy together. It's more selfish for you to keep her on a string while constantly pushing her away, and never giving her a chance to be happy. Why don't you give her the choice? Let her decide what's right for her."

I think she's done, but she opens her mouth again and keeps on talking.

"My brother would not have had a total jerk for his best friend, but the way you're not even giving her a chance to make that choice, by saying no all the time, thinking it's some valiant, self-sacrificing thing. That's bull, Rhett. You're being a jerk. Dusty would hate that." She breaks off, panting, her eyes wide like she's surprised herself. She's sure as hell surprised me. She's so angry.

I try to process all the things she's said.

Me pulling back is being selfish.

I'm keeping Sophie on a string.

Dusty would hate the way I'm acting.

Sophie looks at me like she's in love with me.

I sit there and stare at my best friend's little sister. Could she be right?

THE CAR IS ODDLY silent as Rhett drives us back to Ellie and Asher's house.

I returned from the bathroom to find Rhett and Ellie locked in a stare down over a pile of fries and tomato sauce-covered napkins. As I approached, hesitantly, like you would approach a spooked animal, Ellie pushed away from Rhett, glared at him and disappeared into the crowd. She came back about ten minutes later but has been pretty closed off since.

I asked Rhett what happened, but he shook his head and didn't say anything.

Asher bounces in his seat occasionally, excitedly pointing out a dog we're passing or asking a random question completely out of the blue, but when everyone else's responses are lacklustre he gives up.

Rhett pulls to a stop in the driveway and turns off the car.

Ellie and Asher climb out of the backseat, and while Asher waits for Rhett to get out to say goodbye, Ellie heads straight for the house.

"El!" Rhett calls after her and holds up a hand to Asher, asking him to wait. Rhett chases Ellie up the path, catching up with her as she reaches the porch steps. She turns to face him, her expression undecipherable. He talks to her for a few moments before she nods shakily and reaches out for a hug.

He wraps her up in his arms and they hold on to each other for a long time. When they pull apart Ellie is wiping her eyes.

They turn together and walk back down the path, Rhett heading to Asher to hoist him up and toss him in the air while the little boy giggles.

Ellie comes to me.

"You okay?" I ask her.

She nods, then startles me as she throws her arms around me. She squeezes me tight. "You're so lovely," she whispers in my ear. "I'm sorry Rhett's such an idiot." She pulls away. "Thanks for hanging out with us." Then she spins away, grabs Asher's hand and tugs him up the path behind her as he finishes yelling his goodbyes to Rhett. Aimee meets them at the door, waves to us then tucks her kids away in the house with her.

Rhett turns and climbs back into the car and I do the same.

"Okay if I go change my shirt first? Then we can find some dinner or something?"

"You have room for more food after all those fries?" I ask incredulously.

He laughs. "Not really, no. But I don't really know what else to do. You've put me on the spot."

"Yeah, fair enough," I say. "And of course you can change your shirt. I don't want to be seen with you looking like that."

Rhett laughs, and I'm relieved that whatever happened with Ellie hasn't affected my friendship with him. But then I think about the conversation Ellie started with me. The conversation that thankfully we never quite got around to finishing.

I wonder if she had the same conversation with him and if all the weird tension came from that.

"Is Ellie okay?" I ask abruptly.

Rhett blows out a breath. "Yeah. I think so." He goes quiet, tapping his thumbs against the steering wheel as he drives, and when we stop at an intersection he looks over at me. "I think we're both still adjusting to Dusty not being there." His voice shakes and cracks, and I want to reach out to hug him. I want to soothe away the pain, even though I know I never can.

"She told me you're an idiot," I say, and am relieved when he laughs.

"We both know she's right." His words seem to hold more weight than this simple agreement should.

"Yes, yes we do."

When we arrive at Rhett's house his grandma is in the front garden, spray-painting a huge sheet of plywood a variety of colours. Pastel pink, blue, purple and yellow.

"Hello, Sophie," she says, smiling at me. "I didn't know you were coming over."

"Hi, Grandma," Rhett says before I have a chance to respond. "We've just dropped the kids home and I need a clean shirt." He gestures to his front. "Then is it okay if I hang out with Sophie for a while?"

"Yeah, of course. Don't leave that shirt lying on your bedroom floor. I'll need to get that stain out."

"I wouldn't dream of it," he says. "I'll soak it before we go." Then he places his hand on my lower back and gently leads me inside. He guides me down the hall and enters a bedroom. I stop at the door.

"*This* is your room?" I take in the floral wallpaper, the single bed in the corner with a frilled duvet, the net curtains covering the windows.

"What's wrong with it?"

"Nothing at all. But it doesn't exactly scream Rhett Carmichael, does it?"

He laughs, and it lights up his whole face. He's always been a person who smiles and laughs a lot, but as we've become friends I'm starting to see the difference between the ones he really feels and the ones he just pretends to. "This one's only temporary. One day I'll show you the real one."

I step into the room and try to casually push the door closed behind me. Unfortunately he chooses that moment to pull his shirt over his head, and instead of gently closing the door I fumble and it bangs against the frame.

He looks over at me. My face is hot and probably so, so red.

I knew he was coming in here to change his shirt. I knew that would involve him taking off the one he was already wearing. I did not compute that this would mean he'd be standing in front of me in his bedroom. Shirtless.

He tosses the shirt on his bed and takes a step towards me. He's not laughing now.

"Sweetheart," he says, his voice low. "Why'd you shut the door?"

I gulp. "I told you I wanted to show you something."

He nods slowly and takes another step towards me. "I remember. Not sure what that has to do with closing the door, though."

I shrug, trying for nonchalant and failing miserably.

This is the moment. This is the moment I surprise him; shock him, maybe. Hopefully in the best way.

"I did a thing."

I DON'T KNOW what's happening right now.

Sophie followed me into my room, closing the door behind her. I've never had a girl in my room with the door shut before, and I have absolutely no idea why she closed it.

I step towards her, drawn by some unexplainable magnetic pull. Her face is flushed, cheeks pink, which is one of my favourite looks on her.

She's trying to look me in the eye but her eyes keep drifting lower, over my bare chest, and it makes the twisting feeling in my gut intensify. I'm sure I didn't used to have that sensation in my stomach, but now this weird feeling seems to be there constantly. At least when Sophie is around anyway.

I think about what Ellie said, and I'm starting to believe I'm an even bigger idiot than she implied.

I'm a massive idiot. Like huge. Monumental.

"I did a thing," she says, and lifts the hem of her t-shirt.

My heart stutters and potentially stops.

She doesn't pull her shirt off, but lifts the hem up on one side so I can see the barest edge of her bra. It's candy floss pink. Like her hair.

When I manage to tear my gaze away from the tiniest glimpse of that pink fabric, I can focus on what she's actually showing me.

On her ribcage is a tattoo.

I blow out a breath of astonishment, my eyes flicking up to lock on hers.

"When did you do this?"

"Yesterday afternoon," she says, her voice soft and breathy. It might even be a little shaky. "Tonya took me."

She's looking at me in that way she does when she's not really sure if she's done the right thing, like she did the first time I saw her hair.

"Does your mum know?"

She snorts. "No, of course not."

"Do you like it?"

She bites her lip and my knees almost give out. "I love it."

"Me too," I say, stepping closer and dipping my gaze to study the design.

Detailed in fine lines and the barest touch of dot shading is an open book. Flowers spill out of the pages, bursting into bloom. It's the perfect thing for her.

I feel myself stepping even closer. My hand lifts and brushes across the bare skin below the tattoo. Goosebumps erupt in the wake of my skimming touch.

I look away from the design, meeting her eyes again. "It's perfect," I say. What I really mean is "You're perfect", but those words seem stuck. I don't know where to go from here. I don't know how to deal with this charged moment after building massive walls around my heart all week.

Sophie is the exact length of my forearm away from me. I could let my hand settle and it would rest on her side, moulding to the softness between ribs and hips.

I could do it, but it's probably something I shouldn't do.

What I should do is step away, drop my hand back to my own side, retreat to the far side of the room.

That's what I'd do if Sophie wasn't standing right in front of me, locking her eyes on mine as if willing me to stay.

Ellie's words about the chances of Sophie being interested in me flash through my mind: "And I'm a flying pig."

Monumental idiot.

My hand shifts and Sophie sucks in a breath as my palm makes contact with her side, careful not to press against the new tattoo. One day I'm going to trace every line of it.

But not right now, because in this moment, a split second after my hand curves around her side, Sophie slides her hand around my neck, reaches up and presses her lips against mine.

My breath catches in my throat, and before I have a chance to kiss her back she's pulled away.

She stares at me, wide brown eyes behind those glasses that are both adorable and sexy at the same time. "I'm sorry," she whispers.

I shake my head, dumbfounded, confused. "Why are you sorry?"

"It's not what you wanted," she says. "You didn't want this."

"What? No, sweetheart. I wanted this."

"You did?" Her voice is breathy and filled with hope.

"Yeah, but it wasn't what *you* wanted."

Her expression flickers to one of confusion. We're still standing exactly as we were when she kissed me, my hand against her side, her palm pressed to the back of my neck.

"A perfect first kiss under the stars," I whisper.

"How many times have I told you, the list was really, really stupid?" A smile tugs at the corner of her mouth.

"I don't think I can be the person you need. I don't know that I can be a person who deserves you."

"I don't know who you think you are, Rhett," she says. She swipes her thumb across my skin and I shiver.

"Definitely not the type that makes a good boyfriend. I'm self-ish, grumpy, completely unreliable, no fun to be around." The words spill from me and I wish I was lying to her. I wish I didn't believe them.

"Mmm, yes, because I've never once had a single iota of fun with you." Her voice is teasing, but still, the realities of this situation are coming back to me. The walls she managed to push down for a second with the press of her lips are reforming way too fast.

I try to step away, but she holds onto me. Her free hand reaches out and grabs at the side of my jeans, her firm grip on the fabric holding me in place.

"You told me to get out of my books and live a little. Now it's your turn. Get out of your head. Whatever that stupid, horrible girl said to you, it's not true. You're kind, and generous, and I've had more fun with you than I ever have in my whole, entire life. Okay?"

I stare at her. Her fingertips brush my side as she clutches at me. I want to say she's wrong. I want to agree with her. Before my brain can figure out the correct response, she's talking again.

"Rhett. You're not that person. I promise you. Trust my judgement."

Trust her judgement. Trust her.

I do. I trust her. She's the best person I know and if she sees me that way, who am I to argue?

I nod.

"Good," she says, a split second before she's kissing me again.

sophie

I KISSED RHETT.

I'm kissing Rhett. It's still happening.

In the very first moment my lips touched his, I thought that would be my only chance; my one shot at experiencing what it would be like to kiss him, so I savoured the few seconds I had before pulling away. Rhett was frozen in shock.

But then he told me he wanted it, and now he's kissing me back.

His hand slides around my waist and pulls my body flush against his. His other hand lifts and cradles my jaw, his thumb brushing my cheek, his fingertips resting against my neck.

Both of my arms are wrapped around his neck, my hands tangled in his dark hair.

His tongue brushes my bottom lip and I gasp. Rhett laughs against my mouth and takes a step forward, pressing me back against the door. His hand leaves my cheek, trailing down my neck, fingertips skimming the length of my arm. He slides his hand into mine and weaves our fingers together.

"Are you okay?" he asks, panting slightly as he breaks off the kiss but not pulling more than a few millimetres away. I can feel his words against my cheek.

"More than okay," I manage to say through my disorientation, first from kissing Rhett and then from him stopping so abruptly. "Who needs a starry night."

He's still laughing when I throw myself at him again and I capture the sound with my lips. He tugs at our hands, walking backwards across the room. He sits on the bed, pulling me down so I land sprawled in his lap.

Brushing kisses along my cheekbone he whispers in my ear, "We're not doing anything else, but making out standing up is so much harder."

I shiver, then giggle. The sound is ridiculous to my ears, but there's no other word for it; I definitely giggled.

I readjust my position and find myself eye to eye with Rhett—a novel experience. I lean in and kiss him again. "You're right. This is much easier."

"No crick in either of our necks." He smiles against my mouth, and I melt into him.

His hands roam my back, they run up the outsides of my thighs, they slide up my shoulders, skimming across my throat to cup my face and they tangle in my hair.

My hands do the same, exploring him.

I've never felt more confident, braver, more alive, than in this moment.

Experimentally I press my hands against Rhett's chest and he gives, falling backwards onto the bed. I fall with him, reluctant to break our kissing even for a moment.

A dull thud and a groan from Rhett stops us anyway.

My eyes fly open as I hover above him.

"Ow," he says, then emits another moan. "Wall."

"Oh my god. I'm so sorry," I gasp, sitting properly upright.

He rubs a spot on the back of his head and looks up at me. He cracks up laughing. "You look mortified."

My cheeks flare with heat. "I am," I say, covering my face with both my hands.

"Hey." Rhett reaches up and gently encircles each of my wrists, tugging my hands away from my face. "Don't be. Come here." He applies the slightest pressure and I fall forward again. He adjusts us and I find myself tucked into his side, my head resting against his shoulder, our legs hanging off the side of the bed. "Don't be sorry, don't be embarrassed. If anyone's embarrassed here it should be me for forgetting this is a single bed, which makes the wall so much closer."

I laugh softly, but I'm still embarrassed. My confidence from barely a minute ago has evaporated.

Rhett reaches for my hand, linking our fingers and laying our joined hands across his bare chest. He gives a soft squeeze.

"Why didn't you want to do more than kiss me?" I ask softly, not sure I really want to know the answer.

"No one said I didn't want to. Don't want to." His arm wraps around my waist and I'm fully enclosed by him. I've never felt safer.

"But you said …"

"Soph, sweetheart, it's not that I don't want to, but jumping head first into all that stuff isn't my style. That's no shade to the people that do, but for me, I don't want it to be a heat of the moment thing that we might regret later."

It makes sense, what he's saying. And he's right, I probably would regret it later if I'd ridden that high I was feeling and we ended up doing more.

"This was all out of the blue … well, for me anyway," he continues. "Maybe you had it all planned out how you were going to seduce me."

I laugh, and as I curl into him he presses a kiss against my forehead. "There was no plan," I whisper. "But I don't regret anything."

"Not even whacking my head into a wall? You don't even regret that?"

"Oh, definitely not that part. You needed some sense knocked into you."

"So I've been told."

"Really?" I prop myself up on my elbow so I can look down at him.

"Yeah, Ellie gave me a lecture this afternoon. That's why she was weirdly quiet at the end. She was mad at me."

"Is she still?"

He does an awkward, lying down shrug. "Probably. But she's stuck with me regardless now."

I smile at that. "I'm so happy you all found each other again."

"Me too." He reaches up and tucks my hair behind my ear. "As much as I'd love to stay here, like this, forever," he says, his voice going husky, "we should probably, uh, not be like this when my grandparents come inside. Grandma probably won't be too bad, but jury's out on how Grandad would react. Probably not well."

I look down at him, sprawled on his bed wearing only jeans.

"Speak for yourself. I am perfectly decent."

He laughs. It's his wild and free one. I'm still marvelling at it when he slips a hand behind my neck and pulls me down for another kiss.

We've had a lot of kisses in this short time. Timid and shy, hot and heavy, fast and frantic, long and languid.

This one is soft, but steady.

It's a promise.

SOPHIE and I are in the kitchen when Grandma comes inside. Her face is speckled with spray paint from her canvasses and she's smiling widely.

I take that as a sign that she didn't come inside earlier and find my bedroom door closed.

Grandma offers us a container of cookies, but Sophie groans and shakes her head, placing both hands on her stomach. "I'm way too full," she says.

I grab one and take a huge bite while she stares at me in both horror and awe.

"I don't even want to know how you can eat right now. You ate like four baskets of fries."

"Asher ate most of one of those," I say before taking another bite.

"Oh, and how are little Asher and Ellie?" Grandma says. "I bet they're probably not as little as I remember."

"No, they definitely aren't," I say. "Especially Ellie."

"Always liked that girl," Grandma says. "Never put up with any of your rubbish." She gives me a knowing look.

"Well, that hasn't changed at all," Sophie says, and I shoot her a look, whispering the word "betrayal". She laughs. Grandma does too.

"Right you two, don't let me hold you up. I'm going to wash all this paint off. Have a good time."

She leaves the room, and a moment later water is running in the bathroom.

"Shall we?" I turn to Sophie, reaching out a hand. She nods and slides her hand into mine. Our fingers automatically weave together, like we've been doing this for years, and I lead her outside, down the path and to my car. I stop beside the passenger door and press a kiss to the corner of her mouth. "Do you have an actual plan for this?"

She shakes her head. "No plans. That felt like the point."

"All right then." I open the car door and kiss her again before pulling away and climbing into the driver's seat.

As I pull into the street I reach over and slide my fingers into hers. I rest our joined hands in the space between our seats. Sophie stares down at them, a small smile on her lips.

"Oh!" An idea hits me out of nowhere, and I pull the car over to the side of the road.

"What?" she asks, startled.

"I have an idea."

"Well, I almost had a heart attack. Be less dramatic."

I laugh as I reluctantly release her hand so I can type something into my phone. "That's impossible."

"Oh, I know, but I live in hope."

A couple of weeks ago I thought I had Sophie pegged. I thought I knew all about her and who she was.

But she is constantly surprising me. From blackmailing me, to dyeing her hair pink, to stripping down to her underwear to go swimming with me. The tattoo and kissing me in my bedroom and her smart mouth comments, even though sometimes she looks mortified and sheepish as soon as she's finished saying them, like she can't believe she's been that mean.

I find what I'm looking for on my phone then pull back onto the road, turning at the next intersection.

"Where are we going?" Sophie asks.

I grin at her and reclaim her hand. "It's a surprise. But you'd best prepare yourself."

She eyes me suspiciously but doesn't ask any more questions. Not until we pull into the carpark at the pub.

"You know I'm not eighteen yet, right?"

"I do and it's okay. This place is all ages until ten-thirty tonight."

She surveys the packed carpark and the building that's glowing with various coloured neon lights. When we open the car doors we can hear the music thumping, with bursts of clarity when the pub door is opened.

I slide my arm around Sophie's waist and lead her towards the building. She presses in against my side, almost tucking herself into me.

Once inside, she steps even closer.

"Hey," I murmur in her ear. "You okay?"

Sophie nods, but it's jerky and nervous. "Yeah. It's just a lot. I've never been somewhere like this before."

"I did bring you here for a reason," I say, turning her to face me properly. "But we can leave anytime you want. Okay?"

"Yeah, okay." Her nod is more sure this time. I lean down and brush my lips against hers. She softens further.

I pull away and glance around the room, looking for a free table. I should have known better. There's never a free table in this place on their family nights.

"Yo, Rhett!" A voice shouts across the room and I spot Ricky, Brad and Evan towards the back of the room. Trust them to be here. It shouldn't surprise me; we've spent a lot of hours in this place.

I wave. "You wanna meet my friends properly?"

Sophie's looking nervous again, chewing her lip and pushing her glasses up her nose even though I know they haven't slipped down. But she nods.

I slide my hand into hers, marvelling at how perfect it feels, how natural, and lead her towards the guys.

"It's not like that, huh?" Ricky says as we approach, not even saying hello first.

"Okay, so maybe it's like that now," I say, and he grins at me.

"Good for you." He focusses his attention on Sophie, who once again is pressed into my side. "Hey, Sophie. I'm Ricky."

"Hi," she says, her voice barely audible over the noise.

Evan and Brad introduce themselves and offer her a stool. She slides onto it but doesn't let go of me.

My friends settle into conversation, trying to include Sophie as much as possible, but it's like she shuts down.

Gone is the funny girl with a smart mouth and rebel attitude. We're left with the girl I thought Sophie was before I knew her.

Quiet. Shy. Timid. Scared.

She clutches my hand like a lifeline, like I'm the only thing keeping her afloat.

Brad asks Sophie a direct question and she offers another vague one-word answer. Ricky shoots me a look. I offer him a shrug in return.

I've never seen her quite like this before. Yeah, she was a bit cautious around me at first, but soon enough she was giving me sass like a pro.

She slides off the stool abruptly, stumbling into me a little as she gets her footing.

"Sweetheart," I say, tilting her chin up with my fingers under her jaw. "Are you okay?"

She swallows and nods, a determined glint in her eye a stark contrast to her body language. "Where's the bathroom?"

I point and watch as she weaves her way through the crowd and disappears behind the door.

sophie

I **LEAN** over the sink in the bathroom and study myself in the mirror. I should have known it would come to this. That at some point I'd have to hang out with Rhett's friends, who are a whole group of people I don't know.

I didn't expect it to be tonight. And I sure as heck didn't expect it to be in a country-themed pub that's absolutely packed to the rafters.

It's loud and chaotic and my head is spinning.

The arcade and bowling alley were similar, but they're places full of kids, which made it easier for me to believe they were safe.

This place, though … It's so crowded, there's music pounding and the lighting is all over the place, with bright lights flashing in some areas and the rest of the place in semi-darkness.

I don't know the reason Rhett brought me here, but I know he didn't realise how much it would freak me out.

It's too unexpected, too different from my normal life. That I have no idea why we're here and the whole adventure was totally unplanned is only making it worse.

But I have to deal with this. Especially if I want to be Rhett's girlfriend. Because this is who he is. He's the type of person who exists in bright, loud, people-filled places.

I smooth my hair, take a deep breath and leave the bathroom.

The sound hits me like a slap in the face as soon as I open the door, and I'm disoriented. I scan the crowds, trying to pick out Rhett and his friends, but I'm struggling to see them in the dim light, along with the haze of a smoke machine.

"Oh, Sophie, hey," a voice says beside me. I glance up to find Ricky smiling down at me. "You all good?"

"Uh, yeah. I can't see Rhett."

"We're over this way," he says and leads me through the crowd. Before we arrive at the table Ricky stops me with a hand on my arm, turning me to face him. He leans in and I stiffen.

"This is probably out of line and Rhett will probably kick my ass for it." I try to step back but he's got his hand on my arm. My breath comes short and sharp. I glance around, looking for Rhett. I catch sight of him laughing with Brad and Evan, but he's not looking in this direction. Ricky continues. "But he's been really happy since you guys have been hanging out. I can't really explain how I know, but I do. So thanks for whatever you've done, because he deserves happiness."

Oh. I relax and instantly start silently berating myself for freaking out. I don't know what I was expecting Ricky to do in this room full of people, with Rhett standing right over there.

I smile at Ricky. "Yeah, he does."

"Come on." He turns me with a hand on my shoulder and guides me back to Rhett's side.

Rhett's arm wraps around me and I lean into him. I feel his lips press against my temple and I breathe in the moment. I feel so perfectly safe when I'm with him. I know he's not going to let anything bad happen to me. He's not going to abandon me in this place. He won't leave me behind.

"You all good, sweetheart?" he whispers right next to my ear so I can hear him above the din.

"Yeah," I say, trying to sound way more confident than I feel.

"Good. They're about to start."

"Start what?"

He grins and that spark is there in his eye; the one that lets me know I should be wary. He's up to something. He grabs my hand and leads me away from the table. Ricky and Brad join us and a moment later I find myself in the middle of a space that looks suspiciously like a dance floor. Rhett lines us up to face the stage where a band is preparing to play. Ricky stands on my other side, Brad on the other side of him.

"What's going on?"

Ricky laughs. "You haven't told her?" he asks Rhett.

"Nah, thought I'd surprise her."

"We're line dancing, darlin'," Ricky tells me.

"What? No way!" I back out of the line, but Rhett curls his arm around me and pulls me close to his side before I have the chance to get far.

"It's on your list," he says. "Learn to dance."

"I've told you to drop the stupid list," I grumble. "I can't line dance."

"That's why I brought you here on beginners' night. They walk you through it really slow, then gradually increase the speed of the music as you start picking up the steps."

"How do you even know about this place?"

Rhett shrugs. "We come here every so often."

"For line dancing?" These guys keep surprising me. My overall impression of them definitely wasn't of guys who spend their Saturday nights line dancing.

"Yep," Rhett says. "If you need to, just copy Ricky."

"Why not you?" I ask, suddenly terrified that he's going to leave me here for some reason.

"Because I suck. Like completely. Picture you playing air hockey. That's me trying to line dance."

"Then why do you do it?"

"Because it's fun trying. It's a good laugh, mostly for other people, but still. And tonight, it's because you wanted to learn to dance." I start to shake my head, but he slips his hand into mine. "Sweetheart, you put those things on your list for a reason. Remember how good it felt when you did all the other ones." He presses a kiss against my temple. I think him doing that is my new favourite thing in the whole world.

I take a deep breath, and when I look up Rhett is staring intently at me.

"Okay, I'll try. But I'm going to suck even worse than you."

Rhett laughs. Ricky laughs too. "You don't understand how truly bad he is."

Rhett shrugs like it's no big deal that he comes out to a place filled with people to dance when he can't do it. "Not all of us can be prodigies like you," he says to his friend, his face lit with amusement.

I'm still puzzling over his complete comfort at public humiliation when the MC draws our attention and starts the lesson.

I take a deep breath and prepare myself. I can do this. Maybe.

Rhett squeezes my hand. He believes in me. So why can't I?

SOPHIE IS SO OBVIOUSLY NOT herself right now, and it's not only the line dancing reveal.

Since the moment we stepped inside, she's been on edge. I don't know if it's the venue in general, or if it's that my friends happened to be here, so our date's now kind of morphed into a group hang out, but I was hoping the line dancing would break the tension.

It hasn't.

She's trying—really damn hard—to pretend she's okay. She tells me she's fine when I ask, but she's so closed off, so tense, I'm finding it hard to fully believe her.

When we told her we were line dancing, I expected her to laugh, make a joke about how awful she'd be and then throw herself into it with as much enthusiasm as she has for every other challenge she's set herself.

I didn't expect her face to go pale and her fingers to shake in mine.

I didn't expect her to look like she needs to rush to the bathroom again.

But she stays beside me as the lesson starts, and she tries. She seems to pick up the actual steps fairly easily, but she's so tense it looks like this is some kind of punishment.

Meanwhile, I can't get any of the steps, despite this not being my first time. I stumble my way through though, laughing as the middle-aged woman next to me tries to give me pointers.

"Thanks," I call to her. "But I'm a lost cause," then badly execute a turn.

Ricky, as per usual, is in his groove. He's giving Sophie some pointers as she studiously copies his steps, her bottom lip caught between her teeth. He taps her on the bottom of her chin, flashes her a giant, goofy smile and waves his arms around like they're spaghetti. He begins to overemphasise all his moves, turning them into a parody, and after a moment I notice Sophie's relaxing into her movements ever so slightly.

Ricky glances at me and sticks out his tongue, which makes Sophie glance over her shoulder at me. The barest trace of a smile touches her anxious features.

I'm so relieved. She's starting to relax, to enjoy herself.

Then she trips and stumbles. Ricky and I both reach for her, but neither can catch her in time and she tumbles to the floor.

"Woah, you okay?" Ricky asks, reaching down to help her up.

Sophie stares at him for half a breath, then her gaze flicks to me.

"Sweetheart," I say, putting my hand out since she's clearly pretending Ricky's isn't there. "You okay?"

She pushes to her feet, ignoring both our offers of help. She sidesteps me and rushes into the crowd.

"Go after her," Ricky says with a whack on my shoulder. "She's anxious. I don't think she's good with the crowd. Go make sure she's okay."

I was always intending to follow her, but Ricky's comment about the crowd keeps churning in my head as I weave around people. I catch a flash of white disappearing through the main doors and hope it's Sophie.

I find her outside, leaning against the corner of the building, her arms wrapped tightly across her stomach.

"Sweetheart," I say softly as I approach.

"I'm sorry." She sniffs, then wipes a hand across her cheek. She turns away as I step closer, so I can't see her face.

I tentatively reach towards her, placing a hand on her back. She doesn't pull away, so I inch closer, my arms enclosing her. I'm flooded with relief when she leans into my chest.

"Is there anything I can do?" I whisper into her hair.

She shakes her head.

"Is it the people? Are they too much?"

Sophie stays pressed into my chest, but I feel her nod.

"I'm sorry. I didn't realise." I run a hand down her hair as she sniffles, her arms curled in front of her body like a defence mechanism.

"No," she says, her voice muffled by my shirt. "*I'm* sorry." She pulls back. "I didn't mean to ruin everything."

I place my fingers under her chin and turn her head towards me, tilting her face so I can look her in the eyes. There's a touch of mascara smudged under them and I use my thumbs to gently wipe it away, along with the tears on her cheeks.

"You've ruined nothing," I say. "I promise. But why didn't you say anything?"

"I didn't want it to be a problem," she mutters.

"We've been to the arcade and it hasn't affected you like this. What's different about now?" I pull her close again and am relieved once more when she rests her head against my shoulder.

"I'm not trying to pry, and you don't have to tell me. I'm trying to understand."

"I know," she says with a sigh. "I'm apparently okay with a place filled with kids. Well, okay is relative, I guess." She gives me a watery smile. "I wasn't great there either, but it's easier to cope with. Here, though …" She trails off and lets out a long, heavy breath. "It's dark, it's loud, it's filled with people I don't know, and it's a situation so far outside what I know. It was all a bit much. I'm sorry."

"You don't need to be sorry, sweetheart."

"Yeah, well, neither do you."

Her words cut off the apology I was lining up and instead I laugh softly.

"I've got an idea. A place we can go that's quiet. You keen for that? Or do you want me to take you home?"

"Where's the place?"

I rub the back of my neck, a little nervous to make the suggestion, lest she think I'm suggesting something I'm not. "My place," I say eventually, drawing out the words as if saying them slower will change their meaning. "Like, my actual house, not my grandparents' place."

"Oh," Sophie says softly. "Your parents are away, yeah?"

I nod. "I'm not suggesting anything, except that it's a place we can hang out where you don't have to worry about other people."

"It sounds perfect," she says. "What about your friends?"

I love that she asked about them.

Then, as if she summoned him, the door bursts open behind us and Ricky comes barrelling out, stopping abruptly when he sees us. "Oh, good. You haven't left yet." He holds up my jacket that I'd left hanging over a chair at the table.

Evan and Brad charge out the door behind Ricky, clearly not

realising he's stopped just past the threshold, and the three of them collide. It plays out like it should be on a kids' cartoon.

"Friends? What friends? I don't know those people," I say.

Sophie bursts out laughing, the four of us following suit, and I know in that moment everything will be all right.

46 /
sophie

RHETT DOESN'T SEEM inclined to invite his friends to join us at his place.

He accepts Dusty's jacket from Ricky, still shaking his head and laughing at their clumsy exit of the building.

I'm trying to settle my laughing, but occasionally another giggle bursts out of me. Or worse, a snort.

Ricky reaches out and ruffles my hair as I fail to suppress another laugh. "You all good, Soph?"

I nod. "Yeah, I'm good."

"Awesome." He says it like he already knew my answer. "Where you two cool cats off to now?"

I raise an eyebrow at Rhett. Cool cats? He rolls his eyes.

"We're going to go hang out at his place," I say. "Do you guys want to come?" I hope I'm not overstepping by inviting them to someone else's house.

"You sure?" Brad asks. "You guys don't want to be … uh, alone?"

Rhett rolls his eyes again. "Do we have to invite them?" he says to me, like a petulant child being told to clean his room.

"To be real, I wouldn't invite us either," Ricky says. "Especially not after Brad's question."

I smack Ricky on the arm. "Shut up. Of course you're invited. You could finish teaching me that line dance."

Being outside, away from the pounding music and hazy atmosphere, lit only with the neon glow from the occasional sign, I can think clearly again.

Before I tripped I was on my way to having fun. Hanging out with only Rhett and his friends, without the crowds, will be even better, and I'll be able to actually concentrate on the dance steps.

"You could invite Theo, too," Rhett says, curling an arm around my shoulder and tucking me into his side.

It's a perfect idea. I pull out my phone and type out a message, Rhett relaying his address when Theo replies immediately saying they're coming.

Ricky, Evan and Brad peel off for their own vehicle, and as we approach Rhett's he steps forward and opens the door for me.

"Why, thank you. This is very chivalrous of you."

He laughs, and after I've climbed into my seat he leans in the still-open door and presses his mouth against mine. I sink into the kiss, lifting a hand to weave my fingers into his hair.

"I had an ulterior motive," he says, breaking the kiss and pulling away. "That's never going to get old, you know that, right?"

I blush so hard I think I might catch on fire, but before I manage to make my mind work enough to form a response, he's closed the car door and is rounding the vehicle to his own side.

We drive, holding hands across the centre console, Rhett singing along to whatever rock song is playing on the radio.

Happiness fizzes inside me. The panic from earlier has subsided, and even though I didn't want my anxiety to be a problem tonight—or any other time—I'm not as upset as I thought I'd be when everything finally became too much.

And I knew it would, eventually.

The person Rhett is, I knew he would put me in situations that would trigger it. He wouldn't do it on purpose, but it was going to happen at some point and his reaction, his response—it was perfect.

I feel safe with him, now more than ever. Even Ricky seemed to get it, without us ever having to discuss it. I appreciated his solidarity.

Over the years it's always been easier to avoid the crowds and the chaos of unknown situations, to avoid the parties and sleep-overs, rather than go and be triggered and either have to explain myself or deal with the judgement and ridicule. Or both.

But it's never stopped the yearning to go, to be a part of those things, even though I always gave my mum the impression I didn't care about missing out. That I was happy with things the way they were. I think she was happy to not have to deal with the anxiety attacks too.

Being around Rhett, having Rhett backing me up as I checked off those things on my list … It's meant everything to me, even if he has no idea exactly how much.

He pulls up in front of a two-storey house on the edge of town. It's set back from the road and gravel crunches under the tyres as we head up the driveway.

After parking the car, Rhett leads me up the path to the front door and unlocks it, swinging it wide and gesturing with an arm. "After you." I step inside, Rhett following close behind. "You can snoop around," he says, nudging me forward.

I laugh, but it sounds nervous and awkward.

Rhett shakes his head like it's adorable that I'm so weird. "Come on, I'll show you my favourite spot." He links our hands and tugs me towards the kitchen. It's stunning, with dark blue cabinets and an incredible timber benchtop.

"Wow," I say as I trail my fingers along the raw edge of the breakfast bar.

"It's cool, right?" Rhett says, pausing beside me. "Just never put anything directly on the bench. Like not even a glass of water. My mum will lose all reason if it ever gets a mark on it." He grins, and I can tell it's a family joke.

"I'll try to remember that."

He laughs. "You could probably slice raw meat directly on it and she wouldn't bat an eye." He leans down and whispers directly into my ear. "She's going to love you."

I blush again, and if I keep this up I'm going to need a heavier foundation.

Rhett steps away, leaving cool air in his wake, and I shiver. He slides open a ranchslider and steps onto a deck, beckoning for me to follow. The night isn't particularly cool but the air feels fresh against my cheeks, still bearing the glow of their most recent blush. Rhett leans against the deck railing and I mimic him.

"I love this view," he says, his voice soft.

"It's stunning," I say, leaning into his shoulder. This whole moment is perfect. "What happened over there?" I point towards a section of trees that are dark and bare in the glow of the porch lights. They should be covered with spring growth by now, but there's something not quite right about them.

Rhett stiffens and immediately I know I've asked the wrong thing.

"Ah, there was … a bit of a … fire," he says, turning away. "Come on, the guys will be here soon." He heads back inside, leaving me on the porch, alone.

rhett

IT WOULD BE the perfect time to tell her.

But I don't want to.

No, it's more than that. I can't tell her. I can't stand for her to look at me differently; to know the truth about everything that led me to this point, led me to her. It'll change things.

She'll be disappointed, she'll question if she really knows me, and I can't bear that. Not now, when things are so completely perfect between us.

Thankfully, Ricky, Brad and Evan arrive, barrelling into the living room like a rowdy hurricane, creating the perfect diversion.

Ricky connects his phone to the speaker and blasts out "Cotton-Eye Joe" of all things, but he swears it's the best line dance song. Sophie seems to be appreciating it, laughing along with him as he recaps the steps she was trying to learn at the bar.

There's a knock at the door that I somehow hear over the commotion. I greet Theo and lead them into the melee.

"Of all the things I expected to see in my lifetime," they say, taking in the sight before us, "this is not one of them."

"Agreed," I say. "Drink? Seat? Something else? I'd offer food but I don't actually have any."

Theo laughs. "What kind of party is this if there aren't even snacks?"

"A very impromptu one."

"Theo!" Sophie shouts. "Come dance with me!"

Theo studies me closely for a moment, an eyebrow raised in question. "What did you do to her?"

I raise my hands in surrender. "Nothing, I swear."

Theo laughs. "I like her like this. Don't hurt her." They dance away from me, somehow already knowing the steps to the dance, and fall into step beside Sophie, sandwiching her between them and Ricky.

I fall onto the couch and watch. After two more rounds of the song Sophie and Theo peel away into a corner, puffing from dancing so hard. They glance repeatedly in my direction, and I'm convinced Sophie is updating Theo on today's developments. I grin at them and wave when I next catch them looking.

Ricky plonks himself down next to me. Brad and Evan have made themselves scarce, as if they think we don't know they're off somewhere having a heart-to-heart that will probably end with them making out.

"You know they're talking about you, right?" Ricky says, and I snort.

"Obviously."

"You seem different these past few weeks," he says musingly. "It suits you."

"Uh …" I'm not quite sure what to say to that. Luckily he saves me from having to form a coherent reply by pointing towards the kitchen, where we last saw Evan and Brad.

"Do you think they'll ever tell us?"

"Yeah, eventually. When they're ready. Or maybe not." I shrug. "As long as they're happy."

"Yeah, I suppose. I want to be happy for them, though."

"I'd say it's very little to do with us. Give them time."

"I know." He sighs. "I mean, it took you forever to tell us about Sophie, and it didn't have all the coming out stuff to go along with it." He grins and gives me a friendly shove.

"Oh, shut up," I say, but I'm grinning too.

I grin even more when Sophie heads in my direction and slides straight into my lap, like this is a thing we've been doing forever. Theo sits on the opposite couch and the four of us fall into easy conversation.

Evan and Brad appear in the doorway, a brightly coloured box in Brad's hands.

"Dude, I found these. Got a light?"

I look at the box, and dread curls in my stomach. I'm frozen in place.

Sophie's face lights up. "Fireworks? Cool! Can we?" She turns to me and I can see the excitement in her expression. The others all look keen. How can I tell them no? Setting off fireworks was on Sophie's damn list.

"There's matches up here," Theo stays, standing from the couch and reaching for the little box on the top of the bookshelf.

Ricky and Sophie are standing now too, all five of my friends heading towards the back porch.

Sophie stops by the door. "You coming?" Her voice is so sweet and there's a hint of concern there, as if she knows everything isn't okay.

I can't tell if everything has sped up or slowed down—time, my breathing, my heartbeat.

"Yeah, I'm coming," I say, standing up. But there is absolutely no way I'm letting anyone light fireworks in the backyard tonight.

Flashes of the last time I held that box in my hands light in my memory. The night everything went wrong.

Evan already has one staked in the ground by the time I get

outside. He's holding his hand out to Theo, reaching for the matches.

"No," I call. "Stop!"

Then the front door to the house bangs open and heavy footsteps storm down the hall and into the kitchen.

Grandad stands at the ranchslider, glowering at me.

Oh, this is so, so much worse than I was expecting. I see him take in the group of people and I see the moment his gaze lands on the fireworks.

"Your friends need to leave. Right now," he says, his voice low and lethal. His quiet voice is so much worse than his loud, shouting one.

Theo slides the matches onto the balustrade. "Come on Soph, I'll take you home."

"No," Grandad snaps. "Her mother is on her way. Considering she's been looking for her for the past hour."

Sophie's face drains of colour. She pulls her phone from her pocket, but it doesn't illuminate. "Oh no," she mutters.

Theo gives her a quick hug. "It'll be okay, Soph. I'll wait with you."

Then Ricky, Evan and Brad shuffle past my grandfather, who glares at each of them as they head down the hall.

"Pack this up," Grandad growls, waving a hand towards the fireworks laid out on the lawn. "For God's sake, I can't believe you'd be this stupid, Rhett. As if it wasn't reckless enough the first time, you go and do it again."

I stack the fireworks back into the box, keeping my head down.

"Clearly you didn't learn your lesson last time." He faces me. "Can you imagine what we'd have to deal with if one of your friends had lit one? What the neighbours would say?"

I don't reply. There's nothing I can say that's going to help

♡ 207

right now.

"He said no," Sophie says, appealing to my grandad. "Rhett did, he told us to stop." Her voice is shaking, but I'm so proud of her for standing up to him, even if it's completely pointless.

Grandad grunts, entirely unimpressed.

"It's okay, Sophie," I say to her, as I step past and drop the box onto the outdoor table. "He's right."

"Damn straight I'm right. As if it wasn't bad enough you've already burned down half their trees, you were about to let your friends finish the job."

WOAH.

Rhett burned down the neighbours' trees with fireworks?

Several things click into place at once: His adamant refusal to help me set off fireworks when we originally discussed the list. His weird response when I asked what happened to the trees earlier, and his reaction to Brad and Evan finding the box of fireworks tonight.

Worst of all is that he called me by my real name.

But all those things are wiped from my mind when I see my mum striding down the hallway, clearly having heard exactly what Rhett's grandfather said.

"Sophie," Mum says, her voice tight. "Get your things. We're going home."

"Rhett," I say, reaching out a hand for him. He doesn't move and my fingers trail down the bare skin of his forearm. I'm expecting him to meet me halfway, for our fingers to link and him to squeeze my hand tight. But he lets my fingers drop and suddenly my eyes are burning and I'm worried I might cry.

"Now, Sophie," Mum says, stepping aside so I can head down the hallway.

I glance at Rhett again, but he's averted his eyes and angled his body away. I don't know what's happened. I don't know why he's freezing me out right now.

"Come on, Soph," Theo says at my shoulder. They wrap an arm around my shoulder and lead me towards the front door. I want to look behind me. I'm desperate for Rhett's gaze, but I know I won't find it.

Especially because Mum is marching down the hallway behind us like an armed guard.

I feel like I'm being arrested.

All because my phone died and I didn't notice.

Because for once in my life I was out having fun, having a good time and making friends.

Mum is silent on the drive home. She doesn't speak to me. The car radio is off too, leaving the air hanging heavy and awkward.

I don't know what I can say to make things better, so I don't say anything. I can't text Theo or Rhett until I've had a chance to charge my phone. That's if Rhett even wants to hear from me. He wouldn't even look at me.

I spend the entire ride home staring at my hands, fighting the tears brimming, wondering why he let my hand drop, why he didn't reach out for me, why he didn't catch me.

Something happened. Something to do with him and fire and those trees, but I can't figure out why he didn't tell me when I asked about the trees. Their barren appearance makes sense now, at least.

We pull into the driveway at home and my mum silently gets out of the car and goes inside. I follow her, finding her in the kitchen.

"I'm sorry," I say, because I have to say something. "My phone went flat and I didn't notice."

Mum shakes her head. "Not good enough. You have plenty of

warning of your phone going flat. And I'm sure one of your friends would have had a charger." She curls her lip on the word friends and I don't miss it. It makes me see red, but I'm already in so much trouble.

The truth is though, I've never really been in trouble before, so I'm not exactly sure how this situation is going to play out, what my punishment might be or how I'm supposed to behave.

"I was dancing and the music was loud. I must have missed the low battery warnings."

"You were dancing?" I don't miss the scepticism in her tone.

"Yes. Ricky was teaching me to line dance."

"Ricky?"

"Yes, he's one of Rhett's friends."

"And Rhett is the boy you've been spending all this time with? Including going to his house without his parents home?"

I open my mouth, close it and open it again, but still no words come out. I didn't actually know that was a rule.

Mum raises an eyebrow, waiting for a response.

"It's not like we were alone." My tone is indignant and I'm also purposefully forgetting the time we were there alone, and also the long minutes we were shut in his floral bedroom at his grandparents' house.

Mum sighs, a long, heavy sound, and sits down at the table. "I don't know what's up with you these days, Sophie."

"I—What?"

"The hair, this boy, staying out late, not letting me know where you are."

"How did you find me?" I ask tentatively, not sure I want the answer.

"I rang Tonya, who thought you might be with the boy, so I called his grandparents, who told us where to find you."

I'm not missing her refusal to use Rhett's name.

"Well, I'm sorry my phone died and you worried when you couldn't get hold of me. But I didn't realise that having a life was something I wasn't allowed to do. I thought you'd be happy that I've made friends."

"Don't be snappy at me," Mum snaps right back at me. "I'd be happy if you made friends, but this boy is reckless and you're not to see him anymore."

"What? No! You can't stop me seeing him." Raging fire rises in me. My heart is burning. I won't stop seeing him.

"Don't argue, or I'll take your phone away as well as stopping you seeing him. Now, I think it's time for bed."

I stand there, gaping at her, as she gets up, takes a glass from the cupboard and fills it with water.

"Goodnight, Sophie," she says, her back turned towards me as she stands at the sink.

I huff out a sound of protest but I know it won't do any good, and I can't risk her confiscating my phone too. I spin on my heel and storm down the hall, banging my bedroom door shut behind me.

I flop onto my bed, plugging my phone into the charger the second I'm lying down.

I stare at the screen as the empty battery icon appears, willing it to charge faster. I growl in frustration and toss it onto the bed beside me, even though I've heard you should never leave a charging phone on your bed.

I stomp around the room, throwing my clothes off and roughly pulling pyjamas on. I brush my teeth with fury and by the time I return to my room, my phone is turning on.

A message appears and I hope with everything I have that it's from Rhett.

It's not. It's from Theo. Hoping I'm okay and that Mum wasn't too mad and to let them know what happened.

I wait, but no message from Rhett appears.

I open our message thread. I definitely haven't missed any messages from him.

After an eternity I tap out a message to him and hit send.

Five minutes later there's no reply.

There isn't a reply after half an hour, after two hours, or when I wake up in the morning, my phone still clutched in my hand.

rhett

GRANDAD DOESN'T SAY anything as I clean up the house. He just stands there with his arms crossed, watching me closely.

Luckily the lack of snacks means we made very little mess in the time we were here, and tidying up doesn't take too long. I return the furniture Ricky moved out of the way for his line dancing lesson to its original placement, then I lock the back door and switch off all the lights.

Grandad gestures to his car as he locks the front door behind us.

"But my car …" I wave feebly in its direction at the top of the driveway.

He shakes his head, pointing again to his silver sedan. "I'll put that one away tomorrow. You won't be needing it for a while."

I stare at him, stumbling to a stop on the front path. "What?" He's going to take my car away from me? "But … no. I need it. For school." For driving around aimlessly in the afternoons for a feeble ten minutes before reporting for duty at the book fair, though come to think of it, I haven't been sneaking away in that time recently. In fact, I've been hurrying to get to the warehouse after school so I can see Sophie and spend more time teasing her about her taste in books.

The thought of the lookout flashes through my mind, but I refuse to let that one settle. I refuse to let myself wonder what will happen when I need to go there for a few minutes to breathe, to lift the weight of loss from my shoulders.

Grandad waits, arms folded across his chest once more, until I take a final, wistful look at the black SUV and climb into the passenger seat of his car.

We drive home in silence. I want to ask how I'm going to get to school, but I'm not sure I really want the answer. Maybe Sophie can give me a ride.

I shake my head, clearing the thought.

I'm not particularly surprised things imploded with Sophie the way they did. All I needed was the reminder of who I really am, not the person she thinks I am.

I was kidding myself all along that we were a good match. I knew from the beginning I'm not the type of person she wants to end up with, and I hate myself a bit for getting caught up in her anyway, taking moments from her that I had no right to.

I knew the end was coming before we even started, but I still couldn't stop myself. And I never expected the end to come quite so soon. I thought I'd have a little more time with her.

A little more time to kiss her as much as I wanted. A little more time for her to wrap her arm around me like it belonged there. A little more time for her to look at me with those gorgeous brown eyes filled with happiness and excitement.

I didn't realise it would all come to a crashing end the very day it started.

I follow Grandad inside when we get home, even though it's not really home. Grandma is sitting at the kitchen table, a mug of hot chocolate in front of her. I desperately want to ask for one but I'm too scared she'll tell me no. That I don't deserve one.

"What are you still doing up?" Grandad asks her, his voice softening. "I told you I'd take care of it."

Grandma snorts inelegantly, and a smile tugs at my lips. "Like I'd be able to sleep," she mutters.

Grandad sighs and turns on me, giving me a "see what you've done" look. "Car keys, the keys to your house, phone." He holds out his hand and I stare at his empty palm.

The car keys I was expecting, though how he thinks I'm going to get back to my car, I don't know. It's not exactly walking distance.

What trips me up isn't even his request for my phone. It's the demand for my house keys. To my own home. Admittedly, I haven't really been there since my parents left except for last weekend to mow the lawns, but it was always there and I always had access to it if I needed it.

I wonder if Grandad knows he's taking away the things that feel like lifelines to me. He probably doesn't even realise the significance. Or maybe he does, and he thinks this is suitable punishment.

Punishment for what, I'm not exactly sure.

I was cutting my curfew a little close, but I wasn't out past it. I didn't know there was a rule that I wasn't allowed to go home or have my friends over.

I don't know if Sophie has a curfew and we broke it, or maybe her mum freaked out because she doesn't usually go out on Saturday nights.

Thinking about Sophie is harder than contemplating my impending lack of freedom.

At least I went out on a high, with Sophie in my arms, her breath against my neck as she rested her head on my shoulder and let out a contented, happy sigh. One day, when I can think about all this again, that's the image I'm going to hold on to.

That one, and the one of her standing beside the pool wearing Dusty's jacket, her pink hair bedraggled from the swim, droplets of water on her cheek.

There's a pain in my chest as that image lingers in my mind: the look on Sophie's face as she tried to hold herself with confidence, her insecurity peeking through nevertheless.

I pull my phone and keys from my pockets and hand them over. There's no point fighting this.

The last image I have of Sophie flickers through my mind. The look on her face when her mum arrived, the shock and worry. The quiet way she said my name for the last time; not in a soft, sweet way, but a scared, broken way. And I turned away. I knew the end was coming, so I didn't fight it when it arrived.

I didn't fight for her.

50 /
sophie

FOR THE FIRST TIME EVER, I resent having to be in the library on a Monday morning.

But I'm responsible and conscientious, according to every adult I've ever met, so here I am fulfilling my duties, when I really want to be racing around school until I find Rhett and then make sure he's okay, and hug him for about six years.

I still haven't heard from him. Not a text or phone call or even an email—not that he has my email address, but I've been checking regardless.

My focus continually flicks to the door as I imagine hearing it open and seeing Rhett standing there, wrapped in Dusty's old denim jacket, a sheepish look on his face.

He'll apologise for getting me into trouble.

I'll tell him I don't care. I don't care that my mother thinks she can stop me seeing him. I don't care about anything else but me and him and how he makes me feel like I can do anything, including going to a crowded country-themed bar and line dancing with his friends.

But Rhett never appears at the door. There's no sign of him.

I assumed his grandparents had taken away his phone and

that's why he didn't reach out to me yesterday, so I was waiting for this morning when he would know exactly where I was. He's seen me in the library every Monday morning for weeks now.

My first classes of the day drag on. When I see Theo in second period and they confirm Rhett is at school, my stomach sinks. Something isn't right here.

We have a break between second and third periods, and I head directly for where Rhett usually hangs out with Ricky, Brad and Evan.

I march right up to the picnic table the four of them are sitting around, listening to Brad talking.

"We wanted to tell you…" he's saying. He pauses, shoots a nod and smile at me, and takes a huge breath. "We're together." He gestures to Evan, who's blushing so hard he looks more tomato than human.

Ricky lets out a loud whoop, jumping up from the table. "It's about damn time," he hollers, face split into a huge grin.

"Shh," Brad says, grabbing Ricky by the arm and dragging him back into his seat. "We're not ready for it to be out yet, but we wanted you to know."

"I haven't told my parents," Evan says. "I'm not quite ready for that conversation to go down."

"It's all good, man," Rhett says, reaching over and giving him a friendly cuff on the shoulder. "We're happy for you and glad you finally told us." He grins.

"Finally?" Evan asks.

"Yeah, 'cause we ain't blind, you know," Ricky says. Then he punches Rhett in the arm and nods towards me. "Hey, Soph. You all good?"

I nod. "Thanks for including me," I say to Evan and Brad. "I'm really happy for you."

They both say thank you, then spend some time sharing a look and having a murmured conversation. They both look ridiculously happy.

"Rhett," I say, returning my focus to the reason I marched up here in the first place.

He turns towards me, tilting his chin up so he's looking up at me from his spot at the table. "Hey, Sophie," he says.

No sweetheart. I try not to let that hurt too much.

He makes no move to get up, so I guess he doesn't mind his friends being a part of our conversation.

"Are you okay?" I ask.

He nods. There isn't a trace of his usual grin. There's no laughing or joking, only a solemn nod.

"I haven't heard from you," I say, and I hope it doesn't come out as whiny as it sounds in my head.

"Grandad took my phone ... and my car."

I feel the blood rush from my face. "I'm so sorry. I don't understand. I didn't realise you did anything wrong."

He shrugs like it doesn't matter, but doesn't say anything.

"I thought you'd come and find me this morning." I sound pathetic. It's obvious Rhett doesn't want me here. His friends are shifting uneasily in their seats.

"I was told to stay away from you," he says. "So I did."

"Wha—who told you to stay away from me?"

"Does it matter, Sophie? I'm trying to do the right thing here." His voice takes on an edge of anger, or frustration, or *something*.

"Of course it matters. If it was my mother ... well, she doesn't get that right."

"She's right, swe— Sophie. Listen to her, okay?"

He finally gets up from the table, but he doesn't step towards me like in all the made-up scenarios in my head. Every single way I could imagine this playing out, I never imagined that he'd stand, swing his backpack over one shoulder, send a sad smile in my direction and walk away.

He crosses the courtyard, not looking back, and disappears around the corner of the building.

I stare after him, that sinking feeling from earlier dropping lower and lower, until my heart lies shattered on the concrete at my feet.

I blink back tears. The heat is burning my eyes, but I fight against letting them fall.

Until Ricky is at my side. "I'll talk to him, Soph. He's being ridiculous."

I meet his eyes and finally a tear trickles out. I swipe furiously at it.

"It's fine," I say, my voice trembling and cracking over the two simple words. I suck in a deep breath and steady myself, wiping under my eyes again. "It's fine," I repeat.

Ricky shakes his head. "I don't get it. He's been so happy since he's been hanging out with you. It's kind of sickening."

Evan and Brad chorus agreement.

I shrug. "It doesn't matter. He's made it pretty clear where I stand." Which is not here, at this table, with his friends.

I readjust the strap of my bag. "Thanks for the dance lessons," I say to Ricky. "They were heaps of fun. I'll know all the moves next time I hear 'Cotton-Eye Joe'." He gives me a smile, but it's a bit weak. It matches the one I've got plastered on my face. "And I'm so happy for you two," I say to Evan and Brad, sitting side by side at the table. Their smiles are fractions of what they were earlier and a wave of regret washes over me. I wish I hadn't ruined their moment.

"I'll, um, see you around … I guess," I say, then turn and walk away, straight past the tree Theo and I usually share, hoping I can make it somewhere private before the tears really let loose.

I GUESS it shouldn't be surprising that Sophie came looking for me.

Somehow it is, though.

Maybe I expected that she'd simply accept her mum telling her to stay away from me; that she'd agree and not argue the point.

The Sophie I first met would have done that. She'd have followed the rules and stayed clear.

But I forgot that Sophie from a few weeks ago isn't the same as Sophie now.

Despite her anxiety at being at the bar on Saturday night, she carries herself with a different kind of confidence now.

She has pink hair and a tattoo. Of course she'd seek me out when I totally ghosted her like a complete jerk.

But the reality is, I'm only causing trouble for her. I don't want to cause a rift between Sophie and her mum.

I'm too reckless for Sophie. As much as we managed to gloss over it on Saturday night, I put her in a position that scared her. I hate that I did that.

I also really, really hate what happened with the fireworks and the neighbour's garden. I wasn't intending to commit arson; I only wanted to sit outside on the night of my dead friend's birthday and remember him.

I had a couple of drinks in me from a party I'd been to with my friends. I know my parents thought me going out that night was a bad choice. But I insisted, because apparently I knew better. But at the party I was miserable. I hated watching other people be happy when Dusty was gone. I was angry that he hadn't made it to his eighteenth birthday. That he'd never make it.

Ricky dropped me home, though I was supposed to be staying the night at his place. My parents had taken my absence for the night as an opportunity to go out themselves and weren't yet home. If they'd known I was coming home, they wouldn't have gone out. I know it.

They didn't want me alone on Dusty's birthday.

I found the fireworks that were left over from last year, that my dad had bought on a whim but never got round to setting off.

It seemed like a good way to commemorate Dusty.

Except I was crying too hard when I tried to light them, and I bumped one sideways.

It was too late to save, and when it ignited it shot off in the wrong direct, skimming over the top of the fence and colliding with the stand of native trees in the Delaneys' backyard.

The trees were established and well cared for, like the surrounding gardens. The Delaneys' intellectually disabled son, Charlie, lived with them and cared for the gardens. He spent hours out there.

He always said hello to me when he saw me, and we'd spent a bunch of afternoons playing football on my back lawn. He adored Dusty.

I watched in horror as the firework exploded in the branches of a kōwhai tree, sparks showering the surrounding trees and the tussocky grass planted around the base.

The sparks caught and fire bloomed. I jumped the low fence and ran for the Delaneys' hose, unravelling it as fast as I could and dragging it towards the trees, water spraying everywhere as I sprinted.

The measly garden hose was no match for the fire, though, and the tōtara tree caught next.

A painful scream came from the house and Charlie ran outside in his pyjamas.

"No, no, no, no," he was shouting as he ran towards me. He grabbed for the hose. I fought him for it, trying to angle the water to hit the base of the flames.

It was a losing battle, but Charlie refused to give up. I relaxed my grip, intending to offer him the hose while I called the fire brigade. But he must have been preparing all his strength to rip the hose out of my hands. When I let go he stumbled, right as the fire flared in our direction.

Charlie screamed as the flames met his arm.

I don't know how we'd got so close.

Mr Delaney arrived then, as I was grabbing the hose off the ground and turning it on Charlie.

"The fire brigade is coming," Mr Delaney panted, his face gaunt in the orange fire glow.

I sobbed apology after apology as I held the hose over Charlie's arm, my hand shaking so hard I ended up soaking all three of us. Mr Delaney dragged us away further away from the flames still ravaging the trees.

The fire brigade arrived in a flurry of red lights and the fire was put out.

Charlie was still screaming about his arm and about his trees.

I was still sobbing apologies at anyone who'd hear them.

My parents arrived home after a call from a police officer to half the street standing in our backyard, the fire fighters still hosing down the smoking, skeletal trees.

I explained to my parents, and the police, what had happened, then my parents sent me to bed.

The next morning the smell of smoke was still burned in my nose. I sat on our back porch and stared at what remained of Charlie's garden.

I knocked on the Delaneys' door and apologised, offered to pay for replacement trees and plants and asked after Charlie's injury.

Thankfully, he wasn't badly hurt. But his father was unimpressed with my behaviour and spoke to my parents at length that afternoon, which was the end of me staying at home relatively unsupervised while they went away.

As understanding as they'd always been, even they had to draw the line somewhere. Me burning down their neighbours' backyard and injuring Charlie was that line.

Maybe that'll be the line for Sophie, too. Maybe she needs to know what I did, so she can realise I'm not the person for her.

I sigh and lean back in my seat. The bus I'm on slows down to turn a corner.

No, telling Sophie is only causing more pain for both of us. The easiest way forward here is to let it all go. Maybe one day we can go back to being friends, if she still wants that, and in the meantime, she'll find the person right for her.

Hopefully by then the memory of those few hours when we were together will have faded into a softly focussed blur and it won't hurt quite so much.

Hopefully.

sophie

I STEP inside the book warehouse and almost collide with Rhett's grandma.

"Oh, I'm so sorry," I say, my hand on her shoulder to steady her.

She smiles at me, her eyes crinkling in the corners like Rhett's do. "It's okay, Sophie." She pats my hand. "How are you holding up?"

I blink at her, hoping I've been hit with a stray wave of hay fever or something and I'm not about to cry. "Oh, um, I'm fine."

"Soph!" A voice calls across the room and saves me from having to say anything else. Tonya. I gesture towards her and Rhett's grandma waves me away.

"Hey, what do you need?" I say breathlessly as I hurry across the warehouse to where Tonya is standing, surveying a table with her hands on her hips.

"Oh, nothing. I thought you might need saving."

I laugh. "Um, yeah, thanks."

Tonya rearranges some books. "How're you holding up? How mad is your mum?"

I shrug. I don't really know because I've been avoiding her

since Saturday night. She tried to sit me down yesterday and have a heart to heart, but I managed to dodge it. "Dunno," I mutter.

"And you?" I look up from the book that's caught my eye to find her studying me as intently as I've been studying the book spine.

"I'm fine."

Tonya glances towards the door. "For appearances' sake you're not allowed to work together, but just so we're clear, it's not my choice to enforce that." She winks, then scurries away to stop Trevor trying to pilfer yet another book, leaving me standing there wondering what she's talking about.

Then I turn around and it all falls into place, because Rhett is standing in the doorway staring at me. As soon as our eyes meet he drops his gaze to the floor, taking my stomach with it.

I guess Tonya doesn't know that Rhett's fully supporting my mother's campaign against our relationship. Nice of her to support me though, even if it's pointless without Rhett being interested.

Tonya won't have any appearances to worry about keeping up.

I sigh and head for a table stacked with books waiting to be priced. The book fair starts on Friday, so everything needs to be sorted, priced and displayed by Thursday night. It should all come together, but right now it feels like the entire warehouse is in disarray. Much like my feelings.

I settle down and start stickering books. I should be paying more attention, but I inevitably end up staring across the room to where Rhett is sorting non-fiction books and stacking them into boxes based on sub-genre. He's currently working through some spirituality and self-help books and I wish I could hear his running commentary on each one.

I watch as he pauses before lowering the next book into the

box. He studies the cover, then flips it over and reads the back. He flicks through the pages then sets it aside.

Once he's finished stacking the box he takes the book and catches Tonya's attention. They chat for a moment, gesturing to the book. Then Tonya looks in my direction, like she's talking about me. Rhett glances my way too, catching me in the act of staring.

My cheeks flare and I look away.

I don't understand how we've gone from what we were on Saturday, what we were for the past few weeks, to this, so quickly.

I sigh again, probably for the millionth time today. I sticker a few dozen more books before Tonya collapses into the seat beside me.

"Do you ever sit in a chair normally?" I ask.

"Absolutely not," she says with a chuckle. "This is a far more dramatic way to sit."

I nod my agreement. Got to give her that one.

"I didn't realise things weren't, um, well, going well, I suppose … with Rhett, I mean."

I don't think I've ever heard her sound so awkward. She's always so relaxed about everything.

I shrug. "Seems like Mum told him he has to stay away from me."

Tonya huffs and scowls.

"Apparently Rhett listened."

"I don't even know what you two did wrong."

"Neither do I," I say. "But it's whatever."

Tonya studies me as I ruthlessly attach stickers to book spines with far more aggression than the task requires. "You're going along with her?" She looks like she's about to go fight a dragon on my behalf.

"Rhett is. I didn't have any intention of following her ridiculous rule. Maybe if she had good reason, but there isn't one. Maybe if she'd bothered to talk to me about him or meet him properly. But she didn't." I take a deep breath, the words and emotions pouring out of me. "She didn't bother to ask me what was going on, she's just freaked out because I dyed my hair and met a boy and made some friends. I get why it's shocking, because it's me and I've never done anything remotely interesting before. But it's also really exciting and this whole thing has kind of ruined all of it."

I lie my head on the table, looking up at Tonya, my eyes watery again. Surely the tears are going to dry up at some point? I might shrivel up like a raisin if they keep going the way they have been.

She reaches out and runs her fingers through my hair, fingering the pink ends. "I'll talk to her. She's probably just worried about you. But I think you should talk to her too."

I sit up again, sniffle and wipe at my eyes. "Yeah. I know I need to. Avoidance is so much easier, though."

She laughs. "Yeah, it is. But if you're wanting to prove to her you're okay, and that you're responsible and acting like an adult, then you need to act like an adult. It sucks, but it needs to be done."

I laugh at the face she pulls.

"I've been called responsible all my life. I'm *always* responsible, even now. I never did anything reckless or irresponsible and I'm still being punished."

'Hey." Tonya runs a soothing hand down my spine. "I don't think she means to punish you. I think she's only worried because you've been challenging yourself a lot more recently, and it coincides with meeting Rhett."

I sigh, nodding. "I know. She doesn't understand. But it's not

Rhett leading me astray. He just helped me find the confidence I needed to be the real me."

"You don't seem angry with him?"

I shake my head. "I'm not. I'm sad. But I'm not angry with him."

"Well then, we lo—ah, think he's pretty great for helping you find your confidence." She grins, but I catch her slip, the way she was going to say we *love* Rhett for helping me.

It's sad because it's true.

rhett

IT'S Wednesday lunchtime when Ricky and Theo hold me hostage.

The last few days have been rough, but fine.

Catching a bus to school is totally fine. Catching another one to the book warehouse is also totally fine. Waiting for Grandad to pick us up when we've finished sorting is one hundred percent fine.

It's totally fine when I wake up and the first thing I think about is Sophie. (Honestly, it makes a nice change from always thinking about Dusty first.) It's also totally fine every time I see her at school and she gives me this sad kind of look like she's so disappointed in me.

I'm the first to our usual picnic table at lunchtime, which is strange, because Evan's class prior to lunch is about four metres away but he's nowhere to be seen.

Ricky appears next and sits down opposite me, giving me a chin lift and vague noise in greeting. It's all completely normal until Theo sits down beside Ricky and places a plastic container of food on the table, taking off the lid like they're settling in.

Theo doesn't sit with us at lunch. They don't really acknowledge us much at all. Well, they didn't before Sophie happened, unless we collided in a hallway or something. Then we'd acknowledge we know each other outside of the school gates.

I stare at Theo, then flick my gaze to Ricky, who's busy eating his sandwich in three bites. He's not at all surprised by Theo's arrival. Which means this was planned.

I've been set up.

They continue to eat their lunch like they're not playing me while I try to stare them down across the table.

When Ricky finishes chewing he glances at Theo. "Would you like the honours?"

Theo nods. "Why yes, thank you."

I'm in so much trouble and I don't even know why. "What's going on?" I ask.

Theo holds up a hand, takes another bite and chews, making me wait. "You're a complete and total idiot, Rhett Carmichael."

I blink. And blink again.

"Agreed," Ricky chimes in and I turn my glare on him.

"What is this?" I ask as confusion, and probably all the emotions about Sophie I've been busy suppressing, try to morph into anger.

"Dude," Ricky continues. "What the heck is going on with you? You ditched Sophie like she's nothing."

"Sophie's doing fine. She is, isn't she?" I ask Theo, suddenly afraid that she's putting on a really good front when I'm around.

"Yeah, she is actually. She's sad, but she's okay. But that's not really the point. It's more about you than her right now."

"What about me?" I mutter.

"The fact that you ditched her when you've been so over the top happy with her for weeks. It's the happiest you've been for months, years, eternity," Ricky says.

"Since Dusty got sick," Theo says, and I can't help but flinch at those four simple words, delivered in an even tone.

Silence descends over the table. I stare at the surface, picking at the faded green paint and wondering how so many people have had the chance to scratch their names into it when we sit here every day.

Eventually Ricky breaks the silence. "We don't understand why."

I sigh. The breath that leaves me is heavy. "Because I'm not the person she wants."

"How do you know that?"

"She told me once," I tell Theo. "She once described the kind of person she'd be interested in dating, and it wasn't me."

"Things change," Ricky says with a shrug.

I shake my head. "There's too much in the way. I'm a mess. I'm still totally destroyed over Dusty, I burned down half the neighbour's garden, my ex dumped me because I'm such a disaster and she couldn't handle being around me anymore. I barely know who I am without Dusty. This whole year ... I don't even know who I am anymore."

"There's a lot going on there," Ricky murmurs.

"Yeah." I glance up at my friend and he's watching me with concern in his eyes.

"You say you don't know who you are anymore," Theo says, "so you could be exactly the person Sophie is after and you just don't realise it." They lean back and smack their palms against the table top like they've closed the case.

I shake my head. "It's really not that simple."

"Look, I can't tell you what to do, or who to care about, or how to behave, even though I really wish I could. But you were happy when you were spending time with Sophie. And even more importantly, to me at least, she was happy. Aside from your relationship with Soph, Asher and Ellie will not shut up about you taking them bowling and how much fun they had and also how cute you are with your 'not-girlfriend', which is what they call her."

I crack a smile. In all the drama of Saturday night I'd forgotten about Ellie and Asher. "I really enjoyed seeing them," I say, and Theo gives me a smile then reaches across the table and takes my hand.

"You helped Soph so much, to find her confidence and free herself. But she helped you too. You two are *so good* together. We don't want you to give that up at the first hurdle."

"Her mum not letting her see me is a pretty big hurdle."

"She's making progress with her mum." Theo shrugs. "Give her some time." A long pause is followed by a deep breath. "Also, this might be super out of line, but … after Dusty died my mum saw a grief counsellor for a while. It helped her process everything. If you want it, this is the person's phone number." Theo slides a business card across the table.

"Thanks," I whisper. My voice feels broken. Mum tried to get me to go to one, even before Dusty died, but more so after his death. I couldn't do it. At the time I didn't want to accept that he was gone. She kept trying, but the attempts always fizzled out when I didn't respond. I thought I was doing okay. I thought I was good … until recently. "I've been thinking I might need someone to talk to. I got a referral from my doctor last week, but I might try this one."

"Good. You have us too," Theo says, and Ricky nods.

"You sure do. I didn't know Dusty, but I'm still here if you ever want to talk about him, or anything else." He looks kind of awkward, like he isn't sure how this is all going to be received.

I stand up and round the table until I'm standing right beside where Ricky's sitting. He stares up at me, squinting into the sun. "Get up," I say, giving him a shove.

He stands and I wrap my arms around him.

"Thanks man," I mutter into his shoulder. "Appreciate you."

I TAKE a deep breath before pushing open the door to the kitchen.

"Mum," I say, my voice wary.

She turns from where she's standing at the sink, staring out the window to the darkening backyard. "Yeah, Soph?" She's wary too, and I don't blame her. She's tried talking to me multiple times since the weekend, and I've blown her off every time.

"Can we talk? Like, is now a good time?" My fingers are twisting themselves into knots and my heart is climbing into my throat.

"Of course," Mum says, her voice surprisingly soft. I thought she'd be angry with me, but she's being very gentle as she gestures to the table, then crosses to the pantry and pulls out a packet of Tim Tams. She sets the biscuits on the table before sitting down across the corner of the table from me.

I like that she didn't sit directly opposite. It feels less confronting.

I wait, expecting Mum to start berating me, but she doesn't. She takes a bite of chocolate biscuit and pushes the packet my way.

"I'm sorry," I blurt. "I'm sorry my phone went flat and I made you worry." I take a deep breath, still expecting Mum to jump in with her lecture, but she doesn't, so I continue. "I know I'm not supposed to follow up an apology with a but, but I'm going to.

"I'm not reckless, or acting out, or rebelling, and nothing that has happened has been Rhett's fault. This," I gesture at myself, taking in my hair and one of the outfits Theo helped me put together, "is me being *myself*, and I love it. I love being able to be who I really am."

I glance up at Mum then, dragging my eyes off the woodgrain in the table's surface. Her eyes are a little glossy, but her tiny smile is encouraging. I like that she's letting me talk.

"Rhett," I start again, my voice catching on his name. "He gave me the confidence to try things. When I was with him I somehow stopped being scared all the time."

Whatever I'm planning to say next dies on my tongue as a tear streaks down Mum's face. She presses a hand over her mouth, her eyes never leaving mine.

"Mum, are you okay?" I whisper, a thousand worst-case scenarios flooding my mind. Why is she *crying*?

"I'm sorry, Sophie," she says, voice shaking. "I'm so sorry you needed someone else to give you the confidence to be yourself. I'm sorry I couldn't see it and help you through it. I know you've been happier since you've been friends with Rhett." She takes a shaky breath. "I'm sorry I overreacted on Saturday. I could give you reasons, but they're excuses. I should have trusted you. You've never given me a reason not to."

"I don't think you overreacted," I say. I stand and grab a box of tissues from the corner of the bench, and when I sit again I shift closer to her, wanting to bridge the space between us but not quite sure how. We've never been super affectionate. We're not the "best friends" kind of mother and daughter, despite it being just us. "I was out late and you didn't know where to find me."

"I could have listened to you, but I heard what Rhett's grandfather was saying about the fire and paired it with you acting so differently lately and assumed the worst." Mum pulls several tissues from the box and uses them to wipe her eyes. The tears are flowing more freely now and she's sniffling, too.

God, seeing her cry is the worst.

"Can you tell me about what you've been up to?" she asks finally, stemming the tears. "If you're up for it. I'd like for us to be more open with each other. I want to be someone you can talk to, if you want."

"I want," I say, a smile pulling at my lips as my own tears well.

"Come here," Mum says, abruptly pushing back from the table. The moment I'm on my feet she's crushing me in a hug.

I cling to her, wrapping my arms tight around her as we cry into each other's shoulders.

"You're not allowed to be scandalised, or tell me off," I say hoarsely when we finally pull apart.

She grips my shoulders, holding me at arm's length as her stare bores into me. "What have you done?"

"Nothing I regret," I say.

She takes a long, slow breath. "Hit me with it. There's obviously your hair, and the clothes, which I really like, by the way."

"Rhett took me to an arcade," I say. It sounds so pathetic to say it out loud, like I couldn't do it myself.

Mum gets it, though. "How did that go?"

"It was loud and chaotic and awful, but I had the best time, even though I completely sucked at every single game."

Mum laughs, and I take the encouragement.

"We went bowling, which was also loud and chaotic, but I sucked less. He took me to this line dancing thing, but the crowds were too much there; that's how we ended up at his house on Saturday night."

Mum's hands have turned reassuring on my shoulders, and she gently rubs one.

"I've made friends, not only with Rhett but with his friends as well." I pause, wondering how I tell her about the next one. I figure the best way is to throw it all out there while she's trying to be on her best behaviour. "And I did this," I say, dropping my hand to the hem of my shirt and lifting it to expose the healing tattoo.

I still completely adore it. Every little thing about it, and I don't regret it. I just don't know how she's going to take it.

Mum's eyes widen and she sucks in a gulp of air, but slams her lips closed before any words escape. She exhales slowly, eyes tracing the design.

"It's very you," she says eventually, after what feels like an eternity of my world falling apart. "Do you like it?"

I nod. "I love it." My voice is reverent, like I'm talking about more than just a tattoo.

"Did it hurt?"

A laugh bursts out of me. I was not expecting this. I was expecting this timid truce to crumble to dust at my reveal.

"A little bit," I say, recalling the burn. "But it was worth it."

"The hard and painful things usually are," she whispers. "Sophie, I'm so proud of you."

"What?" The word splutters out of me as shock and confusion ricochet around my body. Proud was not the word I was expecting her to use.

"You figured out who you wanted to be, then did things that scared you so you could be that person. I think it's brave."

The tears are back in my eyes, and this time I have no hope of stopping them before they fall.

Mum pulls me back to her and holds me while I soak the shoulder of her t-shirt.

When the sobs gradually subside, I pull away and Mum shocks me for the hundredth time this evening.

"Do I get to meet Rhett, then?" She's smiling, teasing. "Maybe we can sit down together and come up with some ground rules for your relationship?"

She sounds so hopeful, but I shake my head.

"I don't think so." My voice is still thick with tears and simply hearing his name makes me want to cry all over again.

Mum's face falls. "I'm so sorry, Soph. Is this because of my reaction?"

I shake my head again. "No, Mum, it wasn't you."

Rhett made it clear from the start he didn't think he was boyfriend material. It was me who pushed him to be something more.

He's holding on to so much pain and grief that I can understand where he's coming from. But it's never not going to hurt that at the first hurdle, instead of fighting for me, instead of putting up the tiniest amount of resistance, Rhett walked away.

He made the choice, and it wasn't me.

sophie

I'M SUPPOSED to be at the book fair as soon as possible after school on Friday to help out.

Tonya's been keeping me updated via text so I know it's been chaos all day, with a line forming half an hour before the doors opened this morning and a steady flow of people all day.

We're expecting an after-school rush this afternoon.

But I had another text message this morning too, telling me my order had arrived in-store at the bookshop, so I need to make a detour.

I collect my order and hotfoot it over to the warehouse. The whole street is packed with cars but I find a tiny spot as someone else is leaving.

I carry my bookshop purchase under my arm and hope it's not really weird for me to be bringing brand new books to the charity fundraiser.

Weaving through throngs of people in the warehouse, my heart rate starts picking up and I feel my palms begin to prickle.

I'm not letting my anxiety get the better of me today, though. This place is mine—the warehouse, the book fair—and I'm not letting anxiety take it from me.

I hold onto the feeling I had after I dyed my hair, when I jumped into Aimee's pool, of dancing with Rhett and Ricky to "Cotton-Eye Joe".

I finally make it to the little room at the back of the warehouse where the volunteers can keep their belongings while attending to the chaos on the floor. I shove the door open with my shoulder because it has a tendency to stick.

This time it doesn't stick. It collides hard with something right inside the door.

A grunt lets me know it's a person, most likely a man.

"I'm so sorry," I call through the door, pushing it gently open the rest of the way.

I come face to face with Rhett, who's rubbing a hand over his hip right where the door handle must have got him.

"Hey," he says quietly. "I fixed the door last night. It doesn't stick anymore." He gives me a half-hearted grin. It's a shadow of his usual and my heart twists at the comparison. "Someone really should have made a sign: 'Shoving with your entire body weight no longer required'," he continues.

I can't help myself and a giggle bursts out of me. I slap my hand over my mouth and try to smother it, but all that does is make me snort. I look up from trying to keep myself together to find Rhett watching me with a puzzled look on his face. I don't blame him. It's not that funny. I could have hurt him.

"Are you okay?" I ask. He nods. "I'm glad I saw you," I say, wishing he wasn't watching me with such wariness, like he's not sure I'm going to keep my cool while having a conversation with him. But the reality is he's still my friend, even if I want more and he doesn't.

"I have something for you," I say, heading over to the back corner where Tonya left the box of books I paid for last night, and pull out the box set Tonya showed me on Rhett's first day at the warehouse.

I present it to Rhett.

"What's this?" he asks, dumbfounded.

"It's a box set of *Percy Jackson and the Olympians*. So you don't have to keep getting them out of the library. You can read them whenever you need." I set the books into his hands. He opens and closes his mouth a few times, but doesn't speak. "I also got you this." I hand him the parcel I picked up from the bookshop. "This is a special edition set. In my opinion they're more for looking pretty and being sentimental than for reading, but they're yours, so you can do whatever you want with them."

"You bought me the series?" he asks, voice cracking. "Twice?"

"Yeah." I can feel my blush crawling up my cheeks now that I'm finished my ramblings. I just needed to give them to him and hope I wouldn't cry.

I'm okay with his decision to walk away from us, and my random bouts of crying have definitely settled over the week, but I wasn't sure if I'd be able to handle actually speaking to him.

"Thank you," Rhett whispers, voice shaking. His eyes are wet, like he's on the verge of crying himself.

I clear my throat. "I also wanted to say thank you for the list assist, for everything you did for me. You're never going to understand how much it means to me.

"I—I understand that you don't want to be in a relationship right now, or not with me, or whatever." I wave my hand in the air to emphasise my whatever. "But I want you to know that I wasn't going to listen to anyone else telling me that you weren't right for me. I'm absolutely confident that I know who you are, Rhett. No one else's opinion is going to change how I feel about you.

"You're amazing, kind, generous and so much fun to be

around. You're so special, I thought you should be reminded of that."

I step towards him, stretch up on my tiptoes and press a kiss against his cheek, then turn on my heel and stride back into the warehouse feeling confident and completely in control, maybe for the first time ever.

THE FEELING of Sophie's lips against my cheek lingers as she walks away, leaving the tiny room we've nicknamed the staff room and winding her way back through the crowds, carrying herself with an easy confidence I didn't expect with the number of people in the crowd.

Her words echo through my mind and the books she gave me rest heavily in my hands.

We were only together for a few moments and she's surrounded me in every way.

I want to soak in this moment, hold onto it, never let it go.

But I already did.

I wonder if I would have got another chance.

If I tried.

If I fought for her.

I think about what Theo and Ricky said and what Ellie told me last weekend.

I sit on the floor in the corner of the staffroom and comb over every moment I've shared with Sophie, every conversation I've had with someone else about her, all the thoughts that race through my head and rest on my heart.

I should be out on the floor helping, giving someone else the chance to have a break.

But I sit here and remember the feeling of being with her and how much it reminds me of being around Dusty.

The realisation hits me so hard, even though I should have realised it weeks ago.

Dusty was my best friend. He understood me. He "got" me. It was always comfortable being with him. He was on my side—always—even when I was a total idiot. Sure, he'd call me out and tell me off. But I knew it was because he loved me. He was my person. One of the reasons it was so hard to lose him was because I lost all of that.

And all of that, I get with Sophie. It's not exactly the same. I never wanted to kiss Dusty. I wasn't into him the way I'm into Sophie. But that deep level of comfort, knowing that she's there for me, even when I'm a total jerk. It's the same feeling.

Sophie is also my person.

I'm starting to realise I have more people, too, but the build to this feeling has been more gradual. Ricky, Brad and Evan. Aimee and her husband, Ellie and Asher.

But Sophie.

My mind always goes back to her.

My heart always goes back to her.

I wonder again if she'll give me another chance, but I barely register the thought before I'm rushing through the door and ploughing through the mass of people in the warehouse.

How are there so many people here buying second-hand books?

I weave and dodge, scanning the crowd for a flicker of pink hair, for the pink cardigan she's wearing.

I'm panting from my frantic search but I refuse to give up.

Sophie deserves better than someone who gives up all the damn time, and I am done with that.

Finally, I catch sight of her. She's chatting to a little girl and pointing her in the direction of the children's section. She straightens as the girl skips off and starts talking to a woman beside her who is unmistakably her mother.

I stumble to a stop, but I wasn't fast enough and I'm right in front of them by the time I actually manage to catch my momentum.

"Hi," I say, still panting.

"Rhett," Sophie says, her confusion evident. "Uh, this is my mum. Mum, this is Rhett."

"Hi, Rhett," she says without hesitation. There isn't any kind of disapproving look either, which I take as a good sign. "I owe you an apology. I jumped to conclusions the other night and I'm sorry."

"Uh." I blink at her. I wasn't expecting that reaction. "Thanks. I'm sorry too. We didn't mean to freak you out."

Sophie's mum waves me off. "You didn't do anything wrong. I just need to learn that Sophie's not a panicked little kid anymore."

"Oh, thanks, Mum. I really needed you saying that in front of him." Sophie rolls her eyes but shares a quick smile with her mum. Theo was right. Sophie really was making progress there.

I shake myself free of my confusion, then face Sophie.

"I'm also really sorry for giving up," I say. I probably shouldn't be doing this in front of her mum. I should be doing it some place where it's the two of us so that when I lay my heart on the line and she stomps on it I won't have witnesses.

But maybe this is a way for me to prove to both of them that I'm serious.

"I shouldn't have walked away. I didn't even give you a say."

"I don't need a say. If you don't want to be in a relationship, or whatever we were, that's entirely your call, Rhett. I don't want to force you."

"I know, that's ... I don't know what I meant saying that." I laugh awkwardly. I want to reach out and touch her but shove my hands in my pockets instead.

"The point is, I'm sorry. You've made me happier than I have been in months—years, probably. You're one of my people. You get me. I think I get you. And I shouldn't have given up."

"You're right," Sophie says, but that's it. Nothing more. No indication if what I'm saying is actually helping my case. I'm not even sure what part of what I said she's agreeing with.

"I don't want to lose you," I say, and my voice cracks in the most mortifying way. "I want to do better. I'm seeing a grief counsellor. I'm so messed up. I'm not dealing with Dusty's death as well as I pretended I was."

"I know," she says quietly. Because of course she knew. "I'm really proud of you." She reaches out and her hand wraps around my wrist, giving it a squeeze. I slide my hand out of my pocket and our fingers lace together. I take that as a good sign.

"Is there anything I can do to go back a week and change it?"

"No," she says. "You can't change what happened."

I let out a breath. "Can I fix what I did?"

She smiles. "If you'd let me finish?"

I hadn't realised she wasn't finished speaking, but I mime zipping my lips and gesture for her to continue.

Her smile comes with a little laugh this time. "We can't go back and change it. And I wouldn't want to. I think we both needed this week. You agree?"

I don't want to agree, but I nod. She's right. I needed this week to come to the realisations about Dusty and my own mental state. The realisation that I want to do better, be better, and that I have support around me to achieve that.

"Good," she says. "Then I'm sure we can figure something out." Her smile is as sweet as ever, and her eyes are shining bright as I step forward and scoop her into my arms.

She presses her hands against my back and clings to me, her warmth soaking right through Dusty's old jacket into my heart.

"There will be clear rules in place," her mum calls, and we break apart, laughing. "We'll discuss those later, but I think Tonya might need some help right now."

RHETT and I stand side by side in our hideous high-vis volunteer vests and direct people to what they're looking for, or help them find prices.

Tonya took one look at us standing hand in hand and grinned, then put us to work.

When we aren't helping someone we lean against the wall, our fingers loosely linked by our sides, hidden from view so we don't look like we're completely wrapped up in our own world, even though we totally are.

When someone asks for my help and I slip my fingers from his to move away, Rhett always follows my movement with the tiniest brush of his fingers across my shoulder, arm or lower back, like he can't wait for me to come back to him.

I can't wait to come back to him.

I can't wait until this book sale closes for the day and we can talk this out.

I can't wait to feel his arms wrap around me again and to press my lips against his.

We've got some things to sort out, and Mum's rules to contend with, which will be interesting. And I assume he's still dealing with repercussions from last weekend where his grandad is concerned.

But I'm confident we'll figure it out.

Five o'clock eventually rolls around and Rhett and I fall into step beside the other volunteers, restocking tables and tidying, preparing for another onslaught of readers tomorrow.

"You two go," Tonya says, stopping beside me, a cash box in her hands. "You've done amazing, and we'll give you a full day's work tomorrow and Sunday. But go now. You clearly have better things to be doing."

"Uh, I can't," Rhett says, tilting his head in the direction of his grandparents.

Tonya holds up a finger, a "one minute" gesture. She heads across the room, speaks to his grandparents for a moment, then gives us a thumbs-up before carrying on with her duties.

Rhett squeezes my hand. "I'd better go talk to them."

"Of course. I'll go get my stuff. Do you want me to grab yours too?"

"Yeah, my school bag and those books." He smiles like they're the best thing in the world. "I still can't believe you got them for me."

By the time I've collected our things from the little staffroom, Rhett's grandparents have left.

"I have to be home by eight and they'll review the current situation after they talk to your mum. But Grandma seemed pretty happy about things. She likes you."

We head out to my car and climb in. "Any ideas?"

"Food. Burgers, if that's okay with you," Rhett says.

We buy food and I drive to the lookout without Rhett having to make the suggestion. He squeezes my hand and gives me a soft smile when he realises where I'm going.

We sit on the ledge and watch the day fade as we eat and talk.

There isn't that much to say in the end. Just that we make each other happy, that we're grateful our paths crossed that morning in the library, and again at the book fair. Rhett told me about the fire. I told him about my conversation with Mum and why I've always stayed close and never pushed the limits. I told him about the fear, the panic, the anxiety.

The alarm on my phone goes off at seven-fifteen.

"That's a bit early, isn't it?" Rhett asks, looking down at the screen as he rests his head on my shoulder.

I shake my head. "I wanted to make sure we had enough warning so I had plenty of time to do this."

Then I twist in his arms, lean towards him and press my lips to his. His hand lifts from my waist and tangles in my hair.

I pull away and he groans softly, his eyes still closed.

"I've got another alarm going at seven-thirty, which is when we'll actually have to leave."

"You scheduled kissing time," Rhett laughs. I lean into him, feeling the vibrations of his amusement. "This is the best idea I've ever heard."

Then he catches my mouth with his again.

It's not the perfect first kiss beneath the stars that I once wrote on a whimsical wish list, but it doesn't matter.

This one is better.

acknowledgments

It always feels surreal to write acknowledgements because it means I'm nearly at the end of another publishing journey.

As usual, there are a number of people I need to thank who helped me along the way.

First, my husband Chris and our daughters Charlotte, Taylor and Isabelle. I could not do this without you. Thank you for all of your support, cheerleading and help. Special thanks to Taylor for naming Rhett's favourite donut shop.

Kelsey and Natalie, as always, your support and friendship mean the world to me. Thank you for being you, letting me be me, and for your feedback on the early draft of this book.

Mon: I'm pretty sure this is the book when I started voice-noting you every drafting spiral I had. You lucky thing. Thanks for always talking me out of them, even when I know you're laughing at my dramatics. Also, thank you for your feedback on the manuscript.

Sarah-Elizabeth did a beta read of *The List Assist* and gave me wonderful feedback that made me cry on the golf course. I really appreciate the time and care you took with Sophie and Rhett.

Jenn Rackham once again designed and created the stunning cover for this novel. Her work is outstanding, she's a superstar to work with and I love watching it all come together.

I need to thank Patricia Bell for her editing expertise and skill. The final polish and fine tuning she does is vital to producing a professional quality book.

My author friends always need a shoutout. Thank you so much to everyone who's been on the other end of a voice note or email or DM ready to support, motivate, empathise or have a laugh. Publishing is a crazy ride, and I'm glad to be on it with you.

And finally, to my readers: You're the reason I still get to do this, that I still get to publish books and work towards my author goals. Your support, your love for my books, your enthusiasm and encouragement is what makes the tough days better and the good days great. Thank you so much.

also by lynda tomalin

The Stars Burn Bright

*A sweet, swoony YA romance about discovering and
celebrating your worth.*

Seventeen-year-old Essie is looking forward to
her summer holidays.

It means weeks of dedicating herself to her
sewing business while her parents are busy
working. Sure, her jerk of a brother is home
from university, but he's mostly working too, so
it's easy to stay out of his way. She can be
herself – whoever she wants to be, without
expectation or judgement or always being told she's over-dramatic.

It's going to be amazing.

Until Jackson Sherwood, her brother's childhood friend, comes to stay.

Jax. Essie has no time for the smug jerk who's always smirking at her, like
he's so much better than her.

Jax's arrival threatens to ruin her plans for a peaceful summer, but as their
situation forces them to spend time together, Essie starts to see a hidden
side of the unwanted guest, and starts to learn about herself: who she is,
where she fits in the world … and what she's willing to stand up for.

also by lynda tomalin

Flying and Falling

Hollie is learning to live with depression.

She's working hard to put the darkest days behind her. She's got a job she loves, friends she cares about, and she's coping. In fact, she's doing pretty well.

Then a mysterious – and gorgeous – new boy shows up at school.

Jonathan is running away from his past.

Weighed down by a guilty secret, he's fled to his aunt's rural property under the guise of helping out on the farm.

As Hollie and Jonathan are unexpectedly thrown together, a growing mutual attraction scares and excites them.

But the past isn't so easy to escape, and they both have to decide if it's enough to keep hiding, from themselves and from each other.

Or can they risk hoping for more?

Winner of a Storylines Notable Book Award 2023

Shortlisted for the 2022 Storylines Tessa Duder Award

also by lynda tomalin

Only Ours

The much anticipated spinoff to Flying and Falling.

When Dan and Luke meet through their best friends, sparks fly immediately. The good kind.

For Dan, it's an interesting new development. He hasn't been attracted to a boy before … but this guy is gorgeous.

For Luke, who's still putting his life back together after a terrible accident, it's terrifying.

With four hours distance between them, neither of them thinks anything will happen anyway.

Until they spend a weekend together that could change everything.

But how can Luke move on from his past when he's afraid of being broken again?

And can Dan support Luke, along with everyone else in his life, without losing himself?

Does their fledgling relationship even stand a chance?

about the author

Lynda Tomalin lives in a small town in New Zealand, where she writes sweet, swoony books about teenagers finding their place in the world.

She is a mum of three girls and a farmer's wife, and when she's not daydreaming about her fictional characters and trying to find space for all the books she keeps buying, she works in administration (but mostly only to fund making books).

Find her online:
www.lyndatomalinauthor.com
Instagram and Facebook:
@lynda.tomalin.author

Email:
contact@lyndatomalinauthor.com